# *The*
# BOOK CLASS

*Also by Louis Auchincloss*

FICTION

The Indifferent Children
The Injustice Collectors
Sybil
A Law for the Lion
The Romantic Egoists
The Great World and Timothy Colt
Venus in Sparta
Pursuit of the Prodigal
The House of Five Talents
Portrait in Brownstone
Powers of Attorney
The Rector of Justin
The Embezzler
Tales of Manhattan
A World of Profit
Second Chance
I Come as a Thief
The Partners
The Winthrop Covenant
The Dark Lady
The Country Cousin
The House of the Prophet
The Cat and the King
Watchfires
Narcissa and Other Fables
Exit Lady Masham

NONFICTION

Reflections of a Jacobite
Pioneers and Caretakers
Motiveless Malignity
Edith Wharton
Richelieu
A Writer's Capital
Reading Henry James
Life, Law and Letters
Persons of Consequence: Queen Victoria
and Her Circle

*The*

# BOOK
# CLASS

*Louis Auchincloss*

Boston
HOUGHTON MIFFLIN COMPANY
1984

Copyright © 1984 by Louis Auchincloss

All rights reserved. No part of this work may be reproduced
or transmitted in any form or by any means, electronic or
mechanical, including photocopying and recording, or by
any information storage or retrieval system, except as
may be expressly permitted by the 1976 Copyright Act or
in writing from the publisher. Requests for permission
should be addressed in writing to Houghton Mifflin Company,
2 Park Street, Boston, Massachusetts 02108.

*Library of Congress Cataloging in Publication Data*

Auchincloss, Louis.
The book class.

I. Title.
PS3501.U25B6   1984      813'.54      84-522
ISBN 0-395-36138-9

Printed in the United States of America

S 10 9 8 7 6 5 4 3 2 1

*For My Good Friend*

JAMES W. TUTTLETON

*with my deep appreciation
of his illuminating criticism
of my work*

———————

*The*
# BOOK CLASS

# 1

WOMEN, WOMEN, WOMEN! I am the slave of women, when I am not their buffoon. As if it was not bad enough to be a decorator, ten to twelve hours of the bloody day, obliged to listen to their yowls of dissatisfaction, to exchange and re-exchange acres of chairs, tables and breakfronts, to mix and remix square miles of blinding colors, to create and re-create parlors and dining halls on a scale that would have exhausted a Michelangelo, to smile bravely when a *chef-d'oeuvre* is pronounced "too ghastly," and finally, when one has donned a black tie and escaped, exhausted, into the social fray for a little gin and gossip, to find oneself coupled at dinner with the *other* type, the lawyer in menacing black sequins, the surgeon in blood-red *crêpe de Chine*, and be harangued on the injustices to females of which *my* sex has been guilty!

Of course, it will be argued, because my emotional life has not been notably solaced by the caresses of the fair sex, that I am jaundiced in its respect. But this is not really so. My closest friends and business associates have all been women. Nobody, I am convinced, has been less discriminatory in both his acts and his thinking. If I have a bias, it is in my suspicion that women are intellectually and intuitively superior to men. But I have certainly never thought they were "nicer." And I very much doubt that anyone *could* think so who was raised, as I was, in a society in which the female had so many more privileges than the male. I remember replying, only last winter, to a young woman from my office who was handling my slides for a lecture at the Colony Club, and who, after gazing about in some awe, asked if that noble edifice was indeed a *women's* club.

"Yes, honeybunch, it is. This club was built in the days when women *ran* New York — before they got sidetracked in the dreary *cul-de-sac* of men's jobs!"

Of course, my assistant retorted promptly and vigorously that women today did not want to control their mates by "bedroom wiles" and that, thank you very much, they were quite willing to take their chances in those "dreary" jobs alongside men, and that, boss or no boss, I had just shown myself a prime chauvinist pig!

This may sound impertinent from an employee, but women today feel very strongly about these matters, and in justice to my assistant, I should explain that she had undoubtedly read this paragraph in a profile written by that bitch Rita Stern, this past winter (1979-1980) for *Women's Wear Daily*:

Happy Birthday to Christopher Gates! Our small, sly, sleek, plump, but oh-so-scintillating decorator is sixty. Oh, yes, my dears, he is sixty, *bien comptés*, if he's a day. The little-read but poignantly appreciated author of *vers de société* and spicy *romans à clef*, who finally hit the big league in chintz and lampshades, may seem boyish for his age, but a certain drawn look under those big blue eyes and a few lines in those round red cheeks betray the inroads of the calendar. Chris, who defied the traditions of his blue-blooded banking fore-bears to take a hop, skip and flutter into a trade not usually associated with the stern countenances of ancestral Gateses and Gallatins caused a recent brouhaha at a symposium on Channel 13, when he aired his view that women's lib had cost our sex most of the domestic, economic and political power it had taken our ancestors two thousand years to achieve!

My mistake was in forgetting that persons involved in a crusade lose all sense of humor and proportion. What I was trying to describe at that silly symposium was the remark-able influence exerted by a particular group of American women in a particular place and time. And as that group happened to comprise the women who had dominated my destiny in the formative years of my life, I succumbed to the temptation, prompted, no doubt, by the myriad resent-ments of childhood, to overdramatize my theme. As a result, I have every women's libber in the city down on me.

I was at first amused, then irritated and at last fairly alarmed by the tempest I had aroused. I even began to wonder if it would shatter, not simply the teapot in which it should have been contained, but the whole set of porcelain and the tea party as well. I decided at last that I might have an obligation, not only to the women I had offended, but to myself, to state my contention in exact rather than hyper-bolic terms.

For, to speak soberly — and there are many who would say it is high time — I never meant to offer a serious argu-ment that women in the past, even in *my* past, had any real political or economic clout comparable to what men had. And so it may be incumbent upon me now to try to make an assessment of just what their "power" did consist of and

3 ]

what it contributed to or subtracted from their own welfare. I might do well to take advantage of the milestone of my sixtieth birthday to evaluate what effect on my own anguished self these women had. Was I their victim or their product? Or am I simply their survivor?

In any sociological examination the danger is to select a group so small as to be unrepresentative of anything, or one so large as to be meaningless. My danger will be the first, for I shall not be dealing with the South or with Boston. I shall not even be dealing with the City of New York. I am limiting myself to the skinny island of Manhattan, and to the eastern side of Central Park at that. I shall be dealing with the wives and daughters of the managers of money and industry in New York City, what is sometimes called "society," and I have arbitrarily selected as representatives of this society my mother's "Book Class." These were the dozen women who instituted it as debutantes in 1908 and met every month (except, of course, in the torrid summertime) to discuss a selected title, old or new, until the death of Cornelia Gates sixty-four years later. Even then Mother was not the survivor of the group — there are still three living as I write — but by the time she expired, it was felt that it was too small to go on.

All twelve women were what are now called "wasps." They were white, of course, and had started life as Protestants, although two later became Catholics, and they were "Anglo-Saxon," if that word be stretched, as it is by some, to embrace persons of English, Scottish, German, Scandinavian and Swiss descent. All were listed in the New York Social Register; all were privately educated; all but one were married. Their means were more varied: Justine Bannard, Polly Travers and Mother were born rich; Mylo Jessup and

Leila Lee married rich men; Adeline Bloodgood was almost poor; the others were what was called "comfortable," which in that group, in the nineteen thirties, meant owning an apartment or a brownstone in town, a house in the country, having five or six maids, two to three cars, several clubs and one's children all in private schools. None except Adeline ever held a regular job, although Polly Travers became an Assemblywoman from a district upstate, and several held responsible Red Cross or similar posts during both World Wars.

What to my young observing eyes was most remarkable about the group was the extraordinary amount of service that they received from everyone else. Their mothers, who had grown up just after the Civil War, in an America where servants, though numerous, had not yet, thanks to immigration, become numberless, had been trained to cook and sew and clean, to know, in short, the tasks that they were expected to supervise. But the girls of the Book Class could hardly boil water. They never had to go into the kitchen unless to inspect or give an order; they never had to darn a stocking or make a bed or clean a bathroom. As mothers, they never changed or washed a baby. Everything in the household, from marketing to cleaning, was taken off their hands. The bills were paid by their husbands' secretaries, unless they happened to enjoy keeping a checkbook; all business matters — insurance, taxes, even charitable contributions — were handled "downtown." Never, I earnestly maintain, in the history of the globe has a class of human beings had so little expected of it. Their decks, so to speak, were cleared for action. They floated, magnificently equipped, clean and shining, battleships on a benign sea ready to encounter — well, what but other battleships?

What did they *do*, these princesses of privilege, these battlewagons in a world at peace, with all their endowments? Well, isn't the answer to that precisely the task that I have set myself? I think that all I am going to say at the outset is that they were serious. All twelve women were as serious as a jury drawn up and harangued by a judge at a murder trial. I see them staring at me now, those twenty-four encompassing orbs. Leila Lee — was *she* serious? Yes, even Leila was serious. At least at the start. And at the end, the very end.

Ah, how I envied them! I saw my lot in the doomed faces of males, destined to the gray death-in-life of Wall Street. Perhaps had I been born to a European aristocracy and seen my father and brother in pink coats riding to hounds on a crystal-clear morning, or passing the port around the dining room table while their waiting wives yawned in the drawing room, I might have imagined diversions in a male future. But I could never believe that Father and his fellow officers at the Gallatin Bank really enjoyed themselves — they talked too much about how hard they toiled. It seemed to me that all the fun in life had been left to the wives. When I went in to say good morning to Mother on my way to school, her immunity from the dull routine inflicted on men was emphasized by her still being in bed, with the breakfast tray before her, letters and papers and magazines strewn about, the cook receiving the day's order, perhaps even her secretary writing on her pad, for all the world like Ruth Draper's monologue of the society lady in "The Italian Lesson." And I had a vision of a morning in the back of her green Rolls-Royce, transported from shop to shop to look at beautiful things, with lunch at the Colony Club, or, better still, a French restaurant, an afternoon at a matinee and then home to dress at leisure for a stylish dinner party. Or, if it was a "working day," I saw her at the head of a boardroom table, in a comfortable armchair, receiving reports from a respectful staff about the running of a nursing school or settlement house, and leaving, after some perfunctory votes were taken, with a benign sense of duty well done. I would be envious of my sister, knowing that, when she had completed her dozen years at Miss Chapin's School, she, too, would be eligible for this female existence of multiple delights.

But did these privileged souls ever acknowledge their privileges? Never! That was part of the game. Just as men always emphasized the grimness of their labor (though this, to some extent, may have been true), so did the ladies of the Book Class invariably maintain that they had never a free minute to themselves, that they were expected to be the slaves of their households and offspring, that in entertaining they were constantly encumbered with a required guest list of their husbands' business associates and that vacation resorts were selected for reasons of golf alone. They did not feel sorry for themselves — that was not their note — but they *did* want it known, perhaps in anticipation of the doubt in such an observer as myself, that this life was not all beer and skittles.

What did they look like? Of course, they were all approaching middle age when I first started to observe them critically, but I cannot say that, despite a considerable financial outlay on clothes, they did much to resist its onset. Leila Lee told me once that, at fifty, she was the only member of the group that still remembered she was a woman. Had I been able to mold them into a single female, I think she would have been tall, a bit bony, brown-faced, quick-striding, abrupt and of assertive manners, but always polite to inferiors (those, anyway, who weren't "uppity"), rapid of speech, capable of hearty laughter, and wearing rather bigger jewels than might have been expected. A vulgar observer might have been tempted to use the term "horsy," but it would have been exaggerated.

Their marriages, on the whole, were known as "happy," but it had never been their principle that a man should be snared by lures or that, once secured, he should be retained by any sacrifice of candor or normal deportment. It was a man's duty, if he married at all, to marry within his social sphere, and what was that but the Book Class? One waited; a suitor came. It was the nature of things. And once he had taken the fatal step, well, he had to stick, that was all. Society ordained it. It would be degrading, would it not, for a respectable matron, the mother of a family, to slather her lips with rouge, her cheeks with powder, and swing her hips to induce a man to keep a vow he had already made to God? Of course, there were men who walked out in spite of everything, and others who "made their wives unhappy," the accepted euphemism for adultery, but there was only one divorce among the dozen members of the Class.

As parents, they were — how shall I put it — more human? They gave in here, anyway, to the possessive urge. I think they would all have agreed that a woman's first duty was to her babes. The most loving wife among them was certainly Mylo Jessup, yet Mother used to quote even her as saying, when it was learned that Franklin Roosevelt had been stricken with polio, "How glad Eleanor must have been it wasn't one of her children!" And this sacred obligation to the issue of one's womb was stretched to embrace grandchildren. I have only to reflect on my own past jealousy of small nephews and nieces to gauge the extent of Mother's concern for them.

Of their "public lives," their relation to society in the

small as well as the larger sense, I shall have enough to say later, but I should like now to consider them in action, and how better can I do this than show them at one of their book lunches? I reach into the past for a sample, and the one that jumps to mind is at Mother's on a winter day in Seventieth Street, some time in the mid-nineteen thirties. The book to be discussed is *The Scarlet Letter* — for only in later years did they confine themselves to current produce — and I, home as usual from Chelton School with bronchitis or asthma or even a heart palpitation, am watching covertly from behind the screen before the pantry door, to the amusement of the two waitresses. Our butler, George, who would never have permitted me to eavesdrop, has been temporarily relieved of his duties on Mother's theory that a male presence might clog her guests' ease if a "sexual" topic were to arise.

The ladies have gathered promptly at half-past twelve in the parlor for sherry or tomato juice, and by a quarter to one they are all seated in the dining room. It is agreed, in deference to afternoons presumably crowded, that they will be out by two-thirty. The book will not be discussed until the second course. Soup is for a social "catching up," and the sound, to me behind the screen, comes like a roar. The ladies all talk at once, yet all hear everything that is said. If there is any significant difference between the sexes, it may be that a woman can talk as she listens, while a man hears only himself.

And now, the soup plates removed, a soufflé is served, amid cries of "Oh, Cornelia, one eats too well here!" Hawthorne's masterpiece is introduced by the chairman, Justine Bannard, whose job it has been to "bone up." A few dates and facts are given, and they are off. The voices come to me from across the decades.

I hear Polly Travers, the "politician" of the group. She

9 ]

was born a Wadsworth, of the great upstate landowning family, and she has enjoyed a term in the Assembly in Albany.

"I'm afraid I must confess, Justine, I couldn't get through the book. It may be the penalty of living in such troubled times. When I think of just one day's mail! The countless appeals I have to write to this or that committee of the legislature! I found myself actually envying dear old Hawthorne, who could hole up in Salem and write beautiful prose about a woman taken in adultery. If *that* was all one had to face in a day's work!"

Even behind the screen I can feel the reaction. The Book Class is fatigued by Polly's superior airs, and I wait for Mother to invoke the crushing shade of a father who had been Ambassador to England.

"I don't feel that the classics are all that remote, Polly. I think they have a relevance, even in troubled times. I know that when my father was *en poste* in London during one of the Moroccan crises, he used to read a chapter of *Emma* every night before going to sleep. He maintained that Jane Austen restored his sense of proportion."

"And *I* suggest it's an open question if Hawthorne *is* remote." This is the voice of Georgia Bristed, renowned for her "salon" of journalists and politicians. Like Polly Travers, she is also guilty of condescension. But aren't they all? Doesn't any group with a shared childhood meet for the primary purpose of showing off how much further each has progressed than the others? "Wasn't there a good deal about the Puritans in the Bay Colony to make us think of Germany today? I had the good fortune of getting Dr. Frankel to address a group in my house the other night. He spoke of the horrors of the prison camps. I know people say these are very much exaggerated, but if one tenth of what Frankel told us is true, it's an abomination! For example, he told us that the mayor of his village, who had shown sympathy to a Jewish family, was taken out to . . ."

"Oh, please!" cries Leila Lee. "I can't bear atrocities. Didn't we agree to that, Madame Chairman? No atrocities?"

"That's right, no atrocities, Georgia," Justine Bannard rules, no doubt with a smile.

"All right, all right, if you want to be ostriches!"

"But I think Georgia has a point." I recognize the soft voice of Mylo Jessup, my favorite of the group. "I wonder if we shouldn't discipline ourselves to a certain minimum of horror stories. On Kipling's theory: 'Lest we forget, lest we forget.' We wouldn't want to overdo it, of course. That might be morbid. But shouldn't we dedicate at least one meeting a year to the violation of basic human rights?"

Leila again: "Well, that's fine. Let me know in advance so that I can be sure to skip it. But to get back to *The Scarlet Letter*, have any of you stopped to consider what a ridiculous plot it has? Hester Prynne is married off as a child to an elderly cripple for whom she hasn't a grain of affection. They go to the New World, where he is captured and presumably slaughtered by Indians. Two years later, living alone, without friends or family, she is seduced by a handsome young clergyman, with whom half the women of the town are in love. And for this she is made to stand in the pillory and be ostracized for life! Think, girls, of the city we live in today! I mean, can anyone possibly take seriously a book that tells how a girl is tormented for doing — let's face it — what half the people one knows are doing?"

If, a few minutes before, I could feel the resentment against the State Assemblywoman through the screen, the feeling evoked by Leila's comments almost blows it down. The group will not give her the satisfaction of a rebuttal — the smallest comment might be construed as evidence that her fancied pre-eminence in the sexual game has even been noticed. She must simply be put down. The chairman now handles this. Justine turns Leila's point with a scholarly argument. "I went to the Society Library to look up the question of just what did happen to convicted adulterers in the Bay Colony. I found my answer in John Winthrop's own journal. He records, in the most matter-of-fact fashion, how he sat on a court that condemned a man and woman to be hanged under just these circumstances. One wonders, indeed, if Hawthorne had not read the actual passage."

And now I hear the high, musical tones of the one old maid of the Book Class, Adeline Bloodgood: "Shouldn't we consider what Mr. Hawthorne is trying to *do* with his subject? Surely he knew that a reader in 1850 was not going to agree that Hester should be placed in a pillory. But he knew that she would suffer from a sense of sin, and whether that was because she believed that she had committed a crime — or because the people of her community believed it — or because, being guilty of other sins, she would not dispute for which sin punishment fell — or because, sharing the guilt of original sin, no punishment on this earth could be bad enough — isn't *that* what we should be discussing?"

Dear Adeline! She alone wants to discuss the novel. Perhaps that is why she is an old maid and poor. The Book Class lived in the world — at least in the "great world." It used books as a door. To what? Well, isn't that exactly what I have to find out?

## 2

As I am proposing to constitute myself the historiographer of the Book Class, by direct reporting of my own relations with its members, or by interviews or gossip, or even, as a last resort, by escape to a fiction that will, unfairly, I hope, be dubbed stranger than truth, I should supply my reader with some account of who I am, or, at least, was, or, at the very least, am supposed to have been.

I was born the youngest of three, the ugly duckling in a family of swans, for whom no swanhood was in store. But when I say "ugly," I do not mean of feature — I have always rather fancied my clear skin, my thick blond (now graying) crop of hair and my "innocent" blue eyes. The pejorative term refers only to my size. My brother, Mansfield (called "Manny," in what I always took as a slur upon myself), was straight and tall and beautiful, and my sister, Eleanor, *mutatis mutandis*, his peer. They were youthful replicas of Father and Mother. A cornucopia of success, as in old portraits of heroes, seems to have emptied its rich contents at the feet of the Gates tribe.

Father was president of the Gallatin Bank & Trust Company, as Mother's father, the Ambassador, had been before him. If one had been looking for a family to illustrate a public relations pamphlet to be called "The Best of Wall Street" in the nineteen thirties (a time when such a document would have been sorely needed), ours would have done nicely as a model, with Father looking tall and severe in a morning coat, Mother serene under a wide-brimmed hat, and Manny and Elly in white sports clothes, holding up tennis racquets. We were not as rich as the Rockefellers or Mellons, but we were rich enough to know just how rich they were.

An irreverent stork had deposited me in this exemplary household in 1920. I was what was called an "afterthought" (people don't have them today) and one that Father, in any case, must have often regretted. I was small and frail and bad-tempered. I couldn't have been more than six when my psyche formed the design of retiring behind a hard shell of ill health to protect me from a boys' world that seemed wholly absorbed in throwing balls or hitting them with sticks.

Oh, yes, I was smart enough at a tender age to learn the use of every weapon that I found to hand. If I had not the luck to be born a woman, I could at least be as clever as one. Eleanor had been a bit of a tomboy but only at the age fashionable for such; she had had the wit to switch in time to the far more profitable role of "radiant debutante" and to make an early ally of Father. Manny was stupid enough to be manipulated into an alliance, even by me (though he later proved a perfectly adequate banker), but I decided that I needed something stronger. There remained Mother. Mother was as different from me as day from night, but Mother loved me.

I thus calculated my assets early: Mother and money. The

latter was very evident, even to a child's eye. We lived grandly, with the house on Seventieth Street, the big place on Long Island, the shingle cottage in Maine, the hundred-foot steam yacht. My parents belonged to the sober, publicity-shunning, sedate world of the big bankers and their counsel, a world dominated by the Morgan partners, that tended to regard a bit disdainfully the more flamboyant, or what Mother called "tinselly," society of Newport and Southampton. I am not sure that Father, left to himself and despite his cool demeanor, might not have gone in for these. I was to develop a taste for them myself, preferring a hedonistic attitude towards money to a worshipful one. But that was to come later.

My first real crisis with Father came over boarding school. It was the firm conviction of his and Mother's group that if a boy did not go to a New England boarding school from the age of twelve to eighteen, he would turn into a spineless, effete wastrel, presumably homosexual. But I didn't care; I was determined not to go to Chelton School, where Manny, of course, was football captain, and Father was equally determined that I should. Thanks to my precarious health and Mother's concern about it, I managed to put off the issue for three years, but in the end Father prevailed, and I was packed off, for another three, to the ice and snow, the ringing bells and shouting boys, the grim athletic fields and chanting choirs, the inconsequently beautiful red brick and green lawns of Chelton.

Fortunately, I was able to pit myself against the boys at school much as I had pitted myself against my siblings at home, using a caustic tongue and the diminutive stature that made me largely invulnerable to physical retaliation under a gentlemen's "code," to establish a special position in my form.

I came in the end to be almost grateful for my Chelton training. I think without it I might never have dared to challenge Father to our great duel of wits in 1936.

But before I get to that I must describe my parents, principal actors in our little drama, in more detail. The adjective that may best describe Father is "disappointing." Mansfield Gates was a long, lean, slightly bent man of quiet but imposing presence. He was handsome in a gray, grim way, with small, gray-green, quizzical eyes that could, on rare occasions, twinkle, and in which the beholder might at least try to find a sympathetic light. His hair was short and steel gray; it was flattened down on his scalp so as never to seem out of place, just as his dark suits never showed a wrinkle, nor the lustrous leather of his shoes a smudge. His head was small, like a wading bird's; the fine, regular features immobile; and the watching eyes seemed to anticipate a darting strike, which never came.

Was this then the disappointment? That Father didn't pounce? He didn't pounce, because there was no need: his victims didn't have to be surprised; they were secure in his toils before they were even aware their liberty was threatened. No, where Father fell short of expectations aroused was that he never showed the humanity, or even the humor, that a man of such obvious intelligence, with such a shrewd glint in his eyes, should have shown. His reserve, his pregnant silence and the way he could catch your eye when some duffer was prating on about nothing, stimulated a hope that was dashed when he proceeded — of course, for the most politic reasons — to congratulate the duffer on his perspicacity. Father loved power; he loved Gallatin Bank & Trust; he loved to manipulate people and funds; and he sought to hide the crudeness of his passion behind the sober garb and demeanor of a statesman. He accepted the wildest recklessness of *laissez faire* as a God-given, God-guaranteed economic system, and it is easy to see why the financial pirates of the era unanimously proclaimed him their spokesman and high priest.

Did he love anyone? He treated Mother with a deference and a formal air of affection that many people admired, but in which I read irony; it was evident enough to me that marriage to Cornelia Gallatin had been the keystone to the arch of his ambition. He was never known to be unfaithful, but this perhaps suited his chilly temperament. He may have loved my brother, Manny, his aide and ultimate successor at the bank, but the latter's craven fear and respect for his august sire must have palled at times. My sister Eleanor and he were supposed to be the "lovers" of the family group, but even here I suspected, on both their parts, a bit of a charade: the playing-out to an approving audience of the popular skit of the gruff, adoring, coddled dad and the impassioned daughter who cannot believe (though the smirking onlookers know otherwise) that any Romeo could ever take her from her idol. As for "Baby," as for Christopher, as for dear little me, well, Father and I were on to each other from the beginning. It was a case of mutual, barely concealed dislike.

And yet. All our lives we change, spiritually, physically, in subtle ways, and I can detect today in my shaving mirror aspects of Father's countenance: a certain set look about the lips, a drooping of the eyelids. At first I regarded these signs with dismay, like Dr. Jekyll beholding the eclipse of his own bland countenance by the hateful, hirsute image of Mr. Hyde, but in time I came to feel an odd, perverse pride in them, as if some of my hostility to my progenitor had stemmed simply from my lack of what he had in such abundance, what the military call "command presence," and that my old antagonism might be ebbing with my own belated development of that very quality.

Mother's name, Cornelia, her fine Roman profile and straight, strong figure subjected her to jovial classic allusions than which none was more tiresomely frequent than that to Manny and myself as her "jewels." But in truth Mother's soul had more than a touch of a Roman matron's, and there were times when it seemed almost a pity that she had not more chances to play the heroic. I could see her, to avoid capture by besieging barbarians, serenely handing the poison bowl to Father, determined to quaff herself any remnants that he left. But Seventieth Street in Manhattan was no stage for such elevated conduct, any more than was Westbury, and her natural exuberance, when unchecked by Father, put me in mind of a classic statue on which a wag has placed a derby hat. Mother on the tennis court, sweating freely as she made her effective strokes, her rich chestnut hair falling in unruly tresses about her head, or leaning back on a ballroom chair after too vigorous a hop, stretching her legs out before her and breathing a loud "Phew!," hardly evoked the image of an Agrippina. For this she needed some grand reception where she could make a proper entrance on Father's arm, imperial in pearls and black velvet, with a blue or scarlet ribboned decoration across her breast, holding high her noble head, with its straight beautiful nose and large, candid, blue eyes. Such occasions were rare.

It was natural for people to assume, because she was wealthy in her own right, and came of a distinguished line of forebears, and because she had the voice and demeanor of one accustomed to command, that she dominated her quieter consort, but this was by no means the case. Mother may have been inclined to be bossy with servants, friends and children — she was even at times something of a bully; I have heard her tell a new chauffeur how many blocks she expected him to make to a green light on Park Avenue, and instruct the skipper of our yacht of the best moorings at night — but, like Manny, she was in awe of Father. When her spouse looked at her coldly and said, "Cornelia, your hair is a disgrace — no one would believe you had a maid," she would run back up to her room like a little girl rebuked by a governess. Or if she had showed too high spirits at a party and he reproached her in that same cool tone, adding perhaps that he had been personally mortified, she would retire in abject silence and sometimes, when we saw her next, we would know from her red eyes that she had been weeping.

Mother was naturally noisy, enthusiastic, competitive — and vulnerable. She wanted her children to excel at everything, and although she was loving enough when we were hurt or unhappy — she was a great hugger and kisser — it barely made up for the way she raked us over the coals when she deemed our efforts deficient. She was as devoid of subtlety as she was of imagination: she saw life as a series of games that had to be played with fairness and force. Oh, no, you could never cheat, but you still had to win! Of course, from the beginning I was everything she deplored: puny, sickly, hopeless at sports. I even liked to play with Eleanor's old dolls and learned needlepoint from Mother's French maid! But my sickliness appealed to the deepest pity in the maternal heart. Total opposites, Mother and I loved each other totally from my beginning to her end, a period of over fifty years.

One more word before I get to my duel with Father —

about the setting that my parents created for themselves. A decorator cannot be expected to neglect this. Mother, left to herself, with the aid of all the fine old American pieces of her Gallatin inheritance, could probably not have helped creating distinguished houses. But she was not left to herself. Father had very definite ideas of what the residence of a leading banker should be. His generation was free of the gingerbread vulgarity of the gaudy era of Newport — they all sneered at that — but they weren't really so much better. They could never have told you, for example, why Stanford White was never vulgar and why Horace Trumbauer almost invariably was. They took refuge in Georgian, usually through Delano & Aldrich, and even when their symmetrical, massive red brick edifices were adequately "handsome," they were rarely interesting.

We were Georgian on Seventieth Street and Georgian in Westbury. As I look back, I have a sense of large neat rooms, always clean and fresh (for enough maids could make up even for Mother's disorganization), full of gleaming mahogany, English eighteenth century or American Colonial, sporting prints, duck decoys, splendid silver pieces, George II or III, portraits of the children by fashionable, forgotten artists, and chintz everywhere. If we were spared the vogue (to come later) of American primitives, we were also virgin to any artifacts of note. But Mother and Father, God knew, were not decorating their nests for their future decorator son. They lived in their rather stiff and banal surroundings with perfect content. As I look back at them they seem to be awaiting their ordeal of 1936 like an oddly aristocratic version of Grant Wood's *American Gothic*.

# 3

FATHER hardly even came up to Chelton, but Mother came once a term, and I used to look forward eagerly to her visits. We were allowed to bring four guests to a meal at Parents' House, which was considered a great treat — the food there seeming good to us probably only because it differed from our usual fare — and Mother, whose loud, at times hilarious manner with boys was a great success, added considerably to my prestige in the form. But on a frigid Saturday evening in February of 1936, when she stepped out of her car before Parents' House and I stood on tiptoe to kiss her cold, lowered cheek, I realized at once that something was wrong.

"Please, no boys for supper, darling," she said quickly. "There's something you and I have to talk about."

"What?"

"Let me freshen up. Come back at six. All right?"

In the intervening hour I brooded over what might have happened. It was obviously not a death in the family — I should have had my telegram. Was somebody sick? But why should that be a thing to discuss? I even had a thrilling fore-boding that she and Father might be getting a divorce! There had been no hint of that, but I knew about men's "dangerous age," and was Father not fifty? Three or four boys in my form had parents who were divorced and remarried, and I thought it "chic" to have a mother with a different surname from one's own.

But I discovered, when Mother and I were seated at a table in a far corner of the dining hall, that a very different issue was before me.

"Your father's been having a rather bad time with the tax people."

"You mean with his accountants?"

"No, no. He never has any trouble with people *under* him. It's those terrible government tax people. Auditors, is that what you call them? I suppose they're all socialists or com-munists."

"Now, Mother. One thing at a time. What are they auditing?"

"Well, wouldn't it be his income tax return? They're saying, it seems, that some of his losses weren't really losses. That it was a put-up job."

"What kind of losses?"

"On his Gallatin bank stock. Why, he must have lost more than a million on it!"

"You mean Father *dumped* his Gallatin stock?"

"Not exactly. He needed a loss to balance against his . . ."

"His taxable income?"

"That's it!" Mother exclaimed in relief. "So he sold it to me."

"To *you?* If it was a thing to get rid of, why foist it off on you?"

"Well, you see he couldn't very well sell it to anyone else."

"Why not?"

"Because it was pledged against a loan at Morgan's."

Fortunately, I had been taking a course in economics, in which I had high grades, and, with the help of a few crumpled papers taken from Mother's handbag, I was able to put the story together. Father had assigned to her all of his Gallatin stock, then sitting in a vault at Morgan's as collateral for a loan. Taking her note for its market value, he had then deducted the huge paper loss (the stock was at a low of 40 as opposed to its 1929 high of 350) against his taxable income for the year 1934. He had later taken the stock back by reassignment at the same price, although it had risen considerably in value in the interim. Uncle Sam, understandably, was claiming that the sale and resale were shams and was assessing a deficiency.

"It looks to me as if you had better get ready to pay the deficiency," I opined.

"Oh, but your father has no idea of doing that! He's determined to win the case. That's what's upsetting me. Chauncey Roscoe, his lawyer, is drilling me for the testimony."

"Drilling you?"

"Like a sergeant major! He's teaching me what to say. How I begged your father to sell me that stock because I was afraid Morgan's might foreclose and it would go out of the family!"

I considered this. Why would Morgan's still not be able to foreclose if it had possession of the stock? It would. Mr. Roscoe must have been creating a motive for Mother. *She* would think that her purchase money would be substituted for the stock as collateral, even if it never was and even if

Father had never intended that it should be. So for *her* at least it would have been a real sale.

"But you didn't think that?" I asked.

"I never thought anything at all! Oh, of course, I signed those papers. I always signed everything your father put in front of me. Even if he offered to explain, I'd say, 'No, no, those things are your business.' But when it comes to taking the stand and swearing to tell the truth and nothing but the truth and then reeling off a long spiel of Mr. Roscoe's that I've learned by heart, is that *right*, Chris?"

"By no means."

As I gazed into Mother's stricken eyes and took in the depth of her distress, I think my sixteen years doubled. So *this* was Cornelia the Roman matron! This was the proud lady whose independence and authority I had so envied! The men of Wall Street, I could see, allowed their spouses the appearance of power — oh, yes! — but when it came to a showdown, how summarily were they pulled into obedience, given dotted lines to sign and testimony to learn by rote!

"No matter what Mr. Roscoe says, Ma, when you get on that stand, it's your plain duty to tell the truth. And the truth as nobody but you sees it!" I was much excited, stirred by this sudden, giddying reversal of our usual roles. "You have always taught us that the basic moral choices in life are simple. Well, here you are! Tell Mr. Roscoe that if you are asked to testify, you will say it was your custom in business matters to do as Father told you. And that you knew nothing whatever about the transaction!"

"I'll look like an awful fool."

"That's better than looking like an awful liar."

"Your father will be horribly upset!"

"Well, whose fault is that? Whose idea was this sale, in the first place? Tell him, if you want, that *you*'ll pay the deficiency. You have the money, haven't you?"

"I suppose so. But that's not really the point, Chris. Your father and I have always regarded the money as belonging to both of us."

"Judging from the way he's acted, I'd say he regarded it as belonging to *him*."

"Chris! Don't be disrespectful of your father!"

"Now look here!" I am afraid that my tone soared to shrillness. But I lowered it at once when I saw faces turned to us across the dining room. "You came up here to ask my advice. Very well. You can't treat me as a little boy, then. Choose!"

Mother looked at me strangely for a moment. Then an expression of unfamiliar submission stole over that proud countenance. "That's fair enough, Chris. I couldn't get any help from your brother or sister. They told me to leave it all to the lawyers. That's why I came."

"Good. Now here's what you do. Tell Father that the truth means more to you than any amount of money. If you asked him for a diamond necklace or even another yacht, wouldn't he try to get it for you? You know he would. Well, tell him you don't want anything but *not* to be a perjurer. Tell him the greatest gift he could make you is paying that tax deficiency!"

"Why, Chris, that's beautiful!" Mother exclaimed in astonishment. "And do you know something? I think your father might actually like it!"

"Oh, I doubt that. Father doesn't believe that New Deal tax auditors are entitled to the truth."

"How do you know these things, at your age? That's just the way he put it!"

"Then, don't you see, it's your *duty* to help him do the right thing? You must lead the way!"

Mother embarrassed me before the whole room by leaning over to kiss me on the brow. "My child, you're inspired," she said, almost in awe. "I knew I was right to come up here."

I have never known just what scene took place on Mother's return to New York, for she was afterwards reluctant to talk about it, but she certainly convinced Father and Mr. Roscoe that she would not prove a useful witness, for she was not called. The result of her not testifying, however, or at least what Father and his learned counsel always deemed the result, was nothing short of catastrophic. A large deficiency was assessed against Father, but that was not it. That in itself would have been nothing; Mother and I had already discounted it. But what neither she nor I had anticipated, had even dreamed of, was that Father would be indicted for fraudulent evasion of income tax.

The headlines appalled the downtown world. The president of Gallatin Bank & Trust a criminal! It was a more naïve era. Looking back, I am put in mind of Cagliostro's mystic forecast of the excesses of the French Revolution, made at an aristocratic soirée in Paris. Heads would tumble, the magician predicted, including some of the greatest in the land. "You mean even dukes?" someone asked. "Higher." "Not princes of the blood, surely?" "Higher." "You can't mean . . . !" Ah, but he did — the monarch himself! In Wall Street men looked at each other and wondered if even Mr. J. P. Morgan was safe.

Mother did not telephone me — she was evidently too distraught — but Father did. He was at his best on the wire:

cool, collected, grave, almost friendly. He informed me there was to be a family gathering the following night and that he was sending a car to bring me down from school. He had already spoken to the headmaster. I was to be on the front doorstep of my dormitory at 9 A.M., packed and ready to go. There was no hint of reproach, no bid for sympathy. It was an order, pure and simple.

We sat, the five of us, the following evening at seven, around the long table in the dining room at Seventieth Street under the tranquil indifference of two Sir Thomas Lawrence ladies, magnificent in lace against leafy backgrounds, and a Joshua Reynolds general in scarlet, his hand on a worshipping wolfhound. Mother was flushed and silent; she fingered the silver by her plate nervously. Manny, with his curly red hair and silly boyish grin, looked fumbling and embarrassed; Eleanor, like an extra in an opera, smiled vacantly and made little gestures for show. Only Father was in complete control of himself and the situation.

What I saw that night, for the first time in my life, was the exhibition of naked male power. Oh, I had known it was there, all right, rumbling and muttering in its lair of dirty, dark alleys and high phallic towers somewhere south of Canal Street. It was what had torn me from Mother's arms and pitched me at Chelton; it was what had been invoked by our nurses of old, when we had been *really* naughty and were threatened with a "report to your father." And now here it was! I stood alone on a broad, dark plain, with hushed females shuddering somewhere behind me, a trembling David awaiting the monstrous Goliath whom no miraculous slingshot was going to quell.

Father now explained to us, with admirable clarity and concision, the nature of the legal proceedings brought against him. It was perfectly possible, he admitted, that he might be acquitted on the ground that the transfers of Gallatin stock from him to Mother and from her back to him had been legal and binding transfers, regardless of motive, and that any claim for a resulting tax loss, even if disallowed, could not be deemed criminal. On the other hand, if some New Deal judge, eager to please the party, should incline to a sterner view, it would be a wise defense to prove that Mother, far from being a mere dummy in the transaction, had actively sought to purchase his Gallatin stock for reasons of her own.

"Perhaps I should point out here," he commented parenthetically, "that swaps of stock between husbands and wives for tax write-offs have been entirely customary. No one before this case ever dreamed of its being a crime. We are dealing with an administration in Washington that is determined to persecute its opponents. We must be prepared to take measures appropriate to the situation."

*We!* I pricked up my ears at his pronoun. Why did he so blandly assume that he and I were of one mind? He must have been consciously pushing me, and if he was doing that, had he not recognized that he was dealing with an opponent not to be despised? This was a heady thought, but I was shrewd for my sixteen years, perhaps shrewder than I have ever been since, and I listened now, even more tensely, determined not to be beguiled.

"I want to say right off to you, Chris," Father continued, "that I entirely appreciate that you were trying to help your mother when you and she had that talk up at school. Nothing is ordinarily more important than telling the truth. If it were a simple question of paying some penalty, I should not dream of asking your mother to submit to any coaching in the preparation of her testimony. I should simply say, 'Take

[ 28

the stand, my dear, and tell the truth as you see it!' But unhappily we are faced with a ruthless enemy and the threat of a jail sentence."

"Oh, Mansfield!" Mother cried with a sob. "I can't bear it!"

"I shall expect you to bear anything you have to bear, my dear. We are made of strong stuff, you and I." He continued to address himself to me. "I might feel that even the prospect of jail would not justify the smallest tampering with truth, Chris, if there were no more at stake than myself. But unhappily there *is* more. There is a class, a system, you might even say a whole way of life!"

I saw at once that I should have to drain some of his heavy drama from the scene. "Surely it wouldn't come to prison, Father. Surely we are talking about a fine at most?"

"In this political climate?" Father's frown suggested the iron bars of his imminent confinement. "Don't kid yourself, my boy. The New Deal isn't interested in setting an example to other taxpayers. The New Deal is concerned with permanently disgracing a known leader of Wall Street!"

"What makes you so sure of that?"

"Thirty years of daily experience with the highest echelons of banking and government."

"But not thirty years of experience with New Dealers!"

"Christopher!" Mother cried. "You're being impertinent!"

"Curb your tongue, brat," Manny snarled.

"No, no, I want Christopher to have his say," Father reproved them, seizing the advantage that our discord offered, and I had a mental vision of Claudius in *Hamlet* (we were reading it at school) bidding Gertrude release the angry Laertes. "I want him to face the facts. It's a pity he has to face them so young, but that is not my doing. You may think, Chris, that your old man sits up nights plotting how to do Uncle Sam out of every last penny of his income tax. But it happens that I'm almost as ignorant in these matters as your mother. I leave them to the accountants who take care of my personal affairs so that I may have the time to run my bank. When they came up with the proposal that I sell my Gallatin stock to your mother, it never occurred to me to question it. I doubt that I even thought about it. And now I find myself arbitrarily selected as a whipping boy to discredit the financial community. Do you begin to see now why this case must be won?"

I knew that he was lying about the accountants and that I was about to alienate my whole family, but I found the prospect strangely exhilarating. I had divined that Father's dislike of me could never be overcome and that the splendid sheep for which I should be hanged was worth many times the poor lamb he had taken me for. "Even at the price of having Mother lie under oath?"

"Oh, Christopher, don't be such a priggish bore!" Eleanor hissed.

"The answer is yes, if it were necessary," Father replied coolly. "If Paris was worth a mass, Wall Street may be worth a tergiversation. But, fortunately, it will not come to that. Your mother will simply allow our counsel, Mr. Roscoe, to place a construction on her acts that was perfectly consistent with her deepest loyalties and convictions."

"You mean she won't have to testify?"

"Oh, of course I'll have to testify," Mother intervened impatiently. She had tossed me to the lion! "I shall have to say that I wanted to keep the stock in the family. And I did! What's so terrible about that?"

"Because it's all made up!" I cried. "They're putting words in your mouth!"

Manny and Eleanor both began shouting at me now, and Father watched the fray with a small smile.

"All right, all right!" I shouted back at them. "Have it your way! I bow to the new morality. We tell the truth unless it's dangerous to do so. Fine! I don't want Father to go to jail any more than you do. But I can't help thinking that it would have been more attractive if he'd begged Mother to tell the truth and she'd lied her head off to save him!"

I am convinced that Father never forgave me that to his dying day. Formerly he had merely disliked me. Now he hated me. I had proved he was not a gentleman.

---

I was sent back to school the following morning and did not come home again until the trial. I sat with Manny and Eleanor directly behind our counsel's table and witnessed the admirable scene put on by Mother and Mr. Roscoe. I was almost proud of her!

Our lawyer's bland round pink face seemed always to be repressing a chuckle at anyone's possibly questioning the high motivation of his client.

"Mrs. Gates," he began, facing Mother benignly and touching the tips of his fingers together repeatedly in a gesture that seemed to convey a mild, muted applause, "the common stock of the Gallatin Bank and Trust Company is more to you, is it not, than just another item in your portfolio?"

"It certainly is, Mr. Roscoe," Mother replied in almost too

hearty a tone. "I have always taken a keen interest in the affairs of the Gallatin Bank."

"Did this interest originate with your marriage?"

"No, it preceded it. My interest in the bank, I might say, is lifelong."

"Would you explain that to the gentlemen of the jury?"

Mother turned her gaze on the jury box as a benevolent first lady might take in a group of paraplegic veterans brought to the White House. "My father was president of that bank. *His* father before him had founded it. My grandfather was a nephew of President Jefferson's Secretary of the Treasury. The bank has always been synonymous to me with the highest standards of integrity in business and finance."

"So that when you heard that your husband might have to dispose of a large block of his stock in the bank, you were distressed?"

"I was very much distressed. I had a feeling of almost religious duty about passing on to our posterity every share of Gallatin stock that my husband and I possessed."

"I see. But were you aware that the shares that you purchased from your husband were already pledged as security for a loan?"

"I was."

"Then you must have known that it would have been impossible for your husband to have sold those shares on the market?"

"My husband might have paid off that loan, Mr. Roscoe. We were living in a tight period where anything could happen. I wanted to be sure of that stock. I wanted the purchase money to be substituted for the collateral and that stock turned over to me."

Mother must have been trained for days! She spoke with

remarkable assurance. Now Mr. Roscoe paused, turning away from the witness, a foxy look on his face. He might have been trying to trap her. "If you were so keen on preserving that stock, Mrs. Gates, it strikes me as curious that, having taken such pains to procure it, you should then have sold it back to your husband." He turned back on her suddenly, as if pouncing. "Why did you?"

"Ah, because then the crisis was over!" Mother exclaimed triumphantly. "I knew that he wouldn't sell it *then*. Things were beginning to pick up — all over the country. And I thought it only fitting that the president of Gallatin Bank and Trust Company should be a substantial holder of his own bank's stock!"

"You felt that strongly enough to let him have it at a price well below market?"

"I let him have it for what he had paid *me* for it, Mr. Roscoe. Do you think I wanted to make a profit from my own husband?"

The brilliance of Mr. Roscoe's theory of defense was that it would exonerate Father even if the jury suspected that, so far as *he* was concerned at least, the stock transfers had been a cynical tax fraud. If the jury believed (as they did, in fact) that Mother had bought and sold the Gallatin stock for personal reasons of her own not connected with taxes, then it was perfectly open to Father to claim the tax advantage inherent in the transaction without criminal liability. The beauty of the concept was that the jury was allowed to think as lowly of Father as they chose without being able to convict him! It might have been impossible for Roscoe to save a client whom twelve good men and true thought guilty without the creation of a heroine whom nobody wished to smudge.

And, indeed, that seemed to be the attitude of the United States Attorney. He was very gentle with Mother on cross-examination. It is possible that he did not see the trap that had been set for him. Or he may have been afraid to antagonize the jury by too roughly handling an unhappy woman trying to help her spouse in matters beyond her comprehension. He must have believed, at any rate, that he could convict Father on Father's motivation alone. He failed. Father was acquitted of the criminal charge.

———

So what have I accomplished, in this first study of a crisis in the life of a Book Class member, but to prove the ruthless power of men in upper-class New York of 1936? Father decided what was right and wrong in the eyes of his own dark, inscrutable god, and he made Mother his puppet in placating this deity. This may be perfectly true, but now I come to the aftermath. The whole world, both of Wall Street and the New Deal, *knew* that Father was guilty as charged, and the graven image in the temple was cracked forever. In time people came even to believe that the verdict must have reflected the evidence. Only last winter a lady I sat next to at dinner asked me whether I was any relation to the "famous Mansfield Gates" who had gone to jail in the nineteen thirties!

Why should this have been so, when so many rich couples had been up to their ears in the same kind of tax fraud? Because it was "hung" on Father — that is all. Even on the lips of those who still admired him, the term "buccaneer" (in a friendly sense) came to be substituted for "high priest." His dignity was now generally seen as a kind of pious mask, and one of the grave eyes in the University Club portrait was jovially said to be capable of a vulgar wink. Yet even I must admit that Father accepted this change of atmosphere with heroic passivity. At Westbury he spent more time in his rose garden, and in Seventieth Street with his stamp collection. He withdrew from the world, but so slowly, so imperceptibly, that we awoke in surprise, first to his total retirement and, some years later, to his demise.

And Mother? There had been two heroes in her life, her father and her husband. Now there was only one. But what Father had done was never allowed to give clay feet to the adored statue of his predecessor. Father and Mother continued to lead more or less the same joint life that they had led before, but with a difference. Now they never quarreled. He never reproached her for being loud or messy or late, and if he had, I believe she would have shed no tears.

Mother and I had a tacit understanding for many years that we would not discuss the case. But after Father's death, in 1956, we sometimes did. I was not surprised to discover that she was deeply ashamed of the role she had played. She still felt that she had been right to do what she had done — she would have done it all over again, she insisted stoutly — but she was nonetheless convinced that this did not make her morally right. Such was the puritan in Mother! She believed in a god who would punish her for doing what she *had* to do. A liar was a liar, even if he lied for God. But she loved me for having warned her. Had I not been her favorite child, what I did would have made me it.

## 4

Sixth-form year at Chelton was a time of surprising happiness. I suppose it was typical of me that now that school was almost over I began to find that I liked it. The masters, in view of our pending matriculation, treated us almost as equals; it was a time of philosophic speculation, of serious discussions about life and sex, a period of pause and *recueillement*, when a boy was supposed, as our old headmaster, Dr. Stead, put it, to "find his soul." I discovered that my duties as editor-in-chief of the *Cheltonian* could be largely delegated to fifth-formers eager to succeed me, and I had the leisure to enjoy the small popularity I had gained by my wit and sophistication. I had become at last, despite my small size and athletic incapacity, a kind of "personage" in the school; I had carved out my own little niche among its leaders without conforming to the norm.

I had also mitigated my attitude of distrustful hostility. I had begun to be aware that there could be delights in friendship, and I had made a boon companion of the senior prefect himself, "Chuck" Bannard, my opposite in every respect, a big burly boy, a football hero, of craggy countenance and tousled hair, who had just enough brain to appreciate in me the qualities lacking in his more amiable but less interesting self. Chuck was one of the few boys who were safe from my sarcasm. I felt a curious need to "protect" him, although this may seem ludicrous, in view of our respective positions in the hierarchy. But I had perceived already that school was not going to be all of life.

I had known Chuck before Chelton, as his mother was a great pal of my mother's and a fellow member of the Book Class. Like me, he was a youngest child, but unlike me he was an only son. His mother was supposed to have longed for a boy, and she idolized him, as one could easily see from the way she would reach over to touch him, under the guise of straightening a jacket collar or removing a piece of fluff. These gestures were the more noticeable in that Justine Bannard was naturally an undemonstrative and disciplined woman. Chuck, like most sons, took her admiration for granted, as he basically took her whole, quite fascinating psyche for granted; it would have astonished him to learn that I regarded Mrs. Bannard as a far deeper and more interesting personality than her son. But then I had always been aware, as none of my classmates were aware, that our parents were actually human beings. The Book Class to Chuck, had he ever thought of it, would have been dismissed as a tedious hen party. To me it was always a drama and Justine Bannard a leading lady. I never, thank heaven, felt it profitable or even amusing to don the blinkers of my age and sex.

One of Mrs. Bannard's most noted indulgences was to drive up to Chelton every Saturday on which Chuck played a football game. No other parent that I knew did this, and

I think it was her sense of being conspicuous that made her welcome my presence beside her on the stand. We were soon the best of friends.

Of course, she may have foreseen my uses for Chuck. She may have thought of me as a kind of finishing school for her less sophisticated son, and hoped that I might prepare him against the temptations of Yale. But I think she liked me for myself as well. She may have even recognized that I was mature enough to appreciate a quality in her that Mother and the Book Class were less apt to see: the "matey," almost masculine, response to any true friendliness that glowed beneath the glaze of her rather mocking good manners. Mrs. Bannard was a strong, square woman whose skin was a chalky white and deeply lined; her features were strongly molded; her eyes slate-colored and unfathomable; her tone high, sharp, precise. She sometimes seemed, wearing the big jewels that she so unaffectedly loved, like the caricature of a society woman in a movie, but this effect was soon tempered by the shrewd glance that seemed to beam the question "Oh, you think you're on to *me*, yes, but do you imagine for one moment I don't take *you* in?" It was at such times that one was aware of the genes of her grandfather, reputedly the roughest of old-time mining pioneers, whose fortune had enabled her to afford a marriage to a charming, dilettantish architect of an ancient New York clan who designed exquisite French châteaux for his rich friends — when he felt the urge.

We would sit, she and I, both cozily wrapped in blankets, on the top tier of the grandstand to watch the Saturday game. She would follow the play carefully and knowledgeably, but there was still time for chat. She took a detailed interest in everything about the school, of which her husband was a graduate and trustee. One afternoon, in the half, as she returned the friendly hand wave of the veteran headmaster passing below us, she exclaimed, "If I thought I could be like *that* at eighty, old age would have no terrors."

I glanced to be sure that no one was within earshot. "The years have been less kind with his sermons. He's like Evarts summing up at the impeachment of Andrew Johnson. You remember what the wags said about that?"

She was generous enough not to sneer at my teen-age show-off. "No, Christopher, I don't. What did the wags say?"

"That he was trying to be immortal by being eternal!"

Mrs. Bannard chuckled. "Really, you're outrageous! Is that how you speak of your headmaster? I'm sure Chuck doesn't."

"No, but he listens."

"And everyone says you boys worship Dr. Stead! I suppose we parents live in a fool's paradise. Is there any talk that he may retire?"

"Oh, yes. It is commonly rumored that he will step down on his hundredth birthday."

"But seriously, Chris. Do the boys ever discuss his successor?"

"They say he hasn't been born yet."

"Behave yourself, or I shall tell the Book Class!" Mrs. Bannard and I often joked about the Book Class, which I pretended to hold in awe. "Would the new headmaster have to be a clergyman?"

"I understand there's nothing in the charter about it. But he always has been."

39 ]

" 'Always' is mostly Dr. Stead. I hear Saint Paul's is thinking of changing."

Knowing that she probably had inside information from
the trustees, I concluded that the school was scheduled for a
new head. It did not at that time occur to me to wonder why
a lady of Mother's distant world should be so interested in
the subject. Chelton loomed large to me then; I assumed it
was so with others.

"You think a man of wide culture might do as well as a
priest?" she asked.

"I think almost any man would do as well as a priest," I
quipped, as we turned our attention back to the playing field.

Chuck was properly fond of his doting mother, but like
my brother, Manny, he was in awe only of his male parent,
though what it was that made him jump so to please this
affable and easygoing gentleman I did not know. Certainly
Mr. Bannard was nothing like *my* father. He was a tall,
willowy, handsome man, with the smoothest, sleekest brown
hair, the noblest high brow and the serenest blue eyes. Perhaps
poor Chuck felt that his father saw him too clearly; he may
have divined a merciless gleam in the judgment of the cool
paternal glance, softened though it might be by smiles and
chaffing. Chester Bannard was one of those heirs of fortune
who seemed not only to take for granted that he should strut
in the center of an opulent scene, but that his wife and children should decorously support his performance in minor
roles. He spoke in a kind of drawl, as if he were depreciating
the clever things that he said, even as if there might be something vulgar about cleverness. He was an architect of considerable erudition and excellent taste; he had built some
charming villas. But they were all derivative, usually French
eighteenth century; they had no more "bite," at least in my

far from humble opinion, than the clients who ordered and adored them.

He was building a summer house in Lenox for a Mr. and Mrs. Percy Buck, and he drove over with his clients one weekday morning to show them Chelton School and to take Chuck and me out to lunch. Mr. Buck was a small, dour, balding man, but his wife was one of the most beautiful women I have ever seen, much younger than her husband and tall and graceful, like a Gibson girl. Neither of them seemed to have much to say, but Mr. Bannard kept us all entertained, both at lunch and on our tour of the campus, amusing us with stories about what graduates had paid for which buildings and how they had been flattered into parting with their money. He walked with Mrs. Buck, directing all his remarks to her, calling her attention, with vivid gestures, to this and that. She smiled at him absently but rarely responded. From time to time Mr. Buck, annoyed perhaps at being neglected, would shout something at his wife. Afterwards, Chuck explained to me that she was partly deaf.

"Daddy calls them Beauty and the Beast. Though I don't see that Mr. Buck is so much of a beast. He seems willing enough to pay for his wife's every whim."

"But did you notice how he barked at her?" I demanded indignantly. "She flushed as if she'd been struck!"

Chuck looked surprised. "You minded that, too? Of course, I could see that Daddy did."

"Your father and I are gentlemen."

"I was afraid he was going to say something rude to Mr. Buck."

"And if he had? I think it might have been called for."

"But she's his wife, Chris! Surely it's their affair how they shout at each other."

"*She* didn't shout. Of course, that would have been unthinkable. She's too lovely." When he made no comment, I insisted, "Don't you agree?"

"Oh, she's lovely, sure. But I wish Daddy wouldn't bring beautiful women to school and march them around the campus, where everyone, including Dr. Stead, can see."

I stared. "But her husband was with them."

"Yes, but yards behind, and who would notice him, anyway? Everyone could see that Daddy was making up to her."

"I've never heard anything so puritanical! Have you taken total leave of your senses?"

Chuck turned to me now, frankly agitated. "You don't understand, Chris. Daddy's always had a thing about pretty women, but this time it's going too far. And there's something else at stake, too. Will you swear you won't tell a soul?" Avidly curious, I quickly swore. "There seems to be an idea that Daddy may be the successor to Dr. Stead."

I whistled. "Your old man headmaster? But he's never even been a teacher. And why would he want it? Why would he want to give up architecture?"

"Because he's done all the buildings he wants. He says he's repeating himself. And he's always loved Chelton. Mummie calls it 'a challenge to greatness.'"

Of course, I remembered what Mrs. Bannard had said to me at the football game. I tried to visualize her husband as a headmaster and at last seemed to make it out, or at least as *he* might make it out. He would see himself as a kind of latter-day Arnold of Rugby, dominating a campus of admiring boys, entertaining visiting potentates, leaving dull details to underlings and traveling to Europe during long vacations on his wife's ample income. Yes, I saw it.

"So that's it," I mused. "And you're afraid he may blow

the deal by flirting with a married woman in front of Dr. Stead?"

"Just so."

"Well, if that's the case, we must make him mind his p's and q's."

"But how? That's the point."

"By alerting your mother to Mrs. Buck's visit," I said promptly. "I think we can count on her to do the necessary."

Chuck gazed at me admiringly. "Would *you* tell her? When she comes up next Saturday, for the Pulver game?"

"And how, thank you very much, do you propose that I do that? Shall I greet her with something like 'You should have been here last Wednesday, Mrs. Bannard. You could have loaned your husband a mandolin for his serenade'?"

"No, no, of course not. But you'll find a way. I've seen you with Mother. You two are thick as thieves."

I was pleased with the idea that I should know how to handle his mother, and I felt pleasantly Machiavellian the following Saturday afternoon, after the game, when Mrs. Bannard and I, in the chilly sunset, followed the straggling school across the campus towards the cheerful lights of the dining hall.

"We were honored by a visit from Mr. Bannard this week," I told her.

"I heard he drove over. He's building a house in Lenox."

"A beautiful house, no doubt. If it is to match the beauty of its chatelaine."

"How do you know that Mrs. Buck is beautiful?"

"Because I saw her!"

Mrs. Bannard paused. "You mean she came to school? With my husband?"

"Oh, with hers, too. It was all quite proper."

43 ]

"Well, of course, it was proper! Why on earth would it not be? How long did they stay?"

"Oh, a good part of the day. Mr. Bannard seemed very anxious to show her everything."

"*Her?* Not him?"

"Well, one wasn't so much aware of Mr. Buck. One doesn't notice a man like that when he's trotting around after a couple as striking as his wife and your husband."

She peered at me now, in the darkening air, with a small fixed smile. "Are you trying to tell me something, Christopher Gates?"

"Only that it worried Chuck."

"And not you?"

"Not a bit!"

She nodded decisively. "You're a dear boy, Chris. We must see, between the two of us, that Chuck is never worried!"

She put her arm under mine as we walked into the dining hall, where tea was being served to the faculty, parents and sixth form. I felt as proud as if I had been Lord Nelson escorting Lady Hamilton!

## 5

JUSTINE BANNARD, alone in her compartment on the southward gliding train, watched the straggling Massachusetts villages slip by. On her lap lay a copy of *The Golden Bowl*. The Class on Wednesday would discuss a new life of Henry James, and she was to report on the "late style." She found it fussy and tedious — she liked directness in all things — but she had been interested in the heroine's problem: how to win back a straying husband without blowing the whistle on her stepmother, with whom he was having an affair. Maggie's father's wife had to be spared, or even squared, to save the parental feelings, and the tools normally available to wronged spouses — recrimination, pleading, threats, or even a good old-fashioned "scene" — were not to hand. And just as Maggie had to preserve her father's immunity from scandal, so, Justine resolved, must she now preserve that of the Chelton trustees. She had to fight her battle by being more aware of everything than anyone else.

The trouble was that Chester was not reading Henry James. If Chester was reading any novel, it was more likely

*Anna Karenina.* She knew her husband's tendency, which had intensified with the years, to toy with the romantic concept of the world well lost, to play with the notion of kicking all to ruin — family, friends, profession — and of bolting with a mistress to some Mediterranean or Pacific isle, perhaps even to a joint love death, which, as in *Tristan*, might provide a fitting climax to their high drama. The point would be that tragedy was something rare and fine, reserved for the noble few, while comedy and farce were left for the multitude. And Justine had little doubt in which group Chester placed his wife.

It had taken her many years to realize how fully she had misconceived the character of the man she had married. Chester Bannard from the beginning had looked too much the part of a hero to be one; her error had been in failing to see not that he fell short, but by how much. A world war had contributed to the preservation of her illusions; the vision of a gallant spouse, fighting first as a volunteer with the British, and later, in 1917, with his own countrymen, had mitigated the painful fact of his undisguised interest in other women. Oh, to be sure, he liked her well enough, as he liked the children she bore him and the money she put in his pocket, but he took it all for granted. It was his faith that if a man had good looks and fine taste and guts, the world could not do much better than provide handsomely for him.

After the war, in the nineteen twenties, she had tried to invest in his taste the faith that she had more happily banked in his courage. Chester had started his career in McKim, Mead & White, but had set up on his own after obtaining a small clientele from friends at the Knickerbocker and Racquet Clubs, for whom he constructed Palladian and Georgian villas on Long Island and in Westchester County. But as he did not depend on his profession for his income, and as he loved to travel, fish, hunt and breathe in the air of expensive watering places, he had tended, as the years passed, to pick and choose among potential clients. Justine had come at last to suspect an attrition in his genius, a note of repetition in his designs, a sharper sarcasm in the way he greeted unwelcome examples of the modern school. She began even to wish that he would quit the field before being openly derided as an imitator, a minor R. M. Hunt trying to be a Mansart, a lesser Stanford White trying to be a Brunelleschi.

It was this that had made her clutch to her heart the hope that he might succeed Dr. Stead. He had mentioned the possibility to her in his usual mocking tone, attributing it to the Search Committee's despair of replacing the irreplaceable, but she had at once seen why the trustees might want him. After an administration of fifty years, the school needed a period of pause and breath-taking before the appointment of a vigorous young headmaster with a drastic change of direction, and who could better bridge the gap than a diplomatic and cultivated gentleman of middle age, a graduate as well as a trustee, with no commitments in educational theory to the past or the future? She saw, too, that it might be the saving of their life together. Chelton would be a joint task.

She smiled a bit grimly, three hours later, when the train plunged into the tunnel to Grand Central. Placing *The Golden Bowl* in her reticule, she reflected that she was indeed going to need a Jamesian subtlety to keep Chester from scotching their grand opportunity.

At dinner that night, alone with him in the lovely dining chamber that he had decorated with green panels of Fragonard cherubs, she related the events of her weekend at Chelton.

"You didn't mention that you'd taken the Bucks to the school last Sunday," she ended.

"Didn't I? But you knew I was with them."

"In Lenox, yes. I didn't imagine they'd be interested in seeing a school."

"If you were married to a boor like Buck, you'd be glad of any distraction."

"Is he such a boor?" Justine glanced down at her plate. "I didn't know that."

"Oh, a horror! He sits there, glowering at her. He hasn't the wit to be happy, and he's determined that *she* shan't be. He makes her life a trial."

"Does he beat her?"

Chester, ignoring her irony, continued heatedly: "You know she's deaf, poor creature. But not so much that she can't understand anyone who speaks at all articulately. The brute grunts at her in a voice nobody could make out and then repeats it in a roar. It's as if he slapped her beautiful face!"

"But maybe he only wants to be sure she has heard him! How many husbands care that their wives hear them at all?"

"Is that a reproach? All he has to do is not chew his syllables. He wants to humiliate her, that's what! He can see that she understands every word that *I* utter in a perfectly normal tone."

"Perhaps that's the trouble."

"You mean he's jealous? Well, I hope he is, the clod. Maybe it'll teach him to respect her more!"

"You mean he doesn't respect her now?"

"I'm trying to tell you, Justine, that he's bent on tormenting her!" Chester cried now, in frank exasperation. "He

didn't give a tinker's damn about seeing Chelton; he just
tagged along to spoil the fun."

"Hers or yours?"

"Both, damn it!"

Justine glanced at the pantry door. "Please, Chester, you
needn't use such violent language."

"Well, who brought the subject up?"

"I simply inquired about your trip to Chelton. Was that
a crime?"

"But you knew all about it! You'd been checking up on
me!"

Justine paused, shocked. Never before, in one of his "inter-
ludes," had he shown such temper. "You strike me as being
very protective of Mrs. Buck."

"Mrs. Buck is a damsel in distress! Like Andromeda, she's
chained to a rock."

"And you're Perseus?"

"Let's just put it that I'm concerned."

She felt a bleak wind in her heart. Uncharacteristically, she
let herself be reckless. Henry James and *The Golden Bowl*
went out the window. "Chester, you're in love!" she exclaimed in a low voice.

"Put it that way, if you wish."

"I don't wish. But you are, and what's more, it's the first
time!"

"I don't want to talk about it," he muttered morosely.
"There's no point discussing these things. One's hit or one's
not hit. It's nobody's fault."

The butler came in with the roast, and they managed to
talk of other things. But her sense that she was faced with a
situation more dangerous than previous episodes was con-

firmed by his curt refusal to discuss it after dinner. In earlier attachments he had paid her the dubious compliment of making her a confidante; indeed, he had seemed to regard his freedom to discuss the virtues — and faults — of the lady he happened currently to admire as one of the pleasures attached to a wandering fancy. But there had been no such note in his reference to Amelie Buck.

Later that night, after their lights were out and she had been sleepless for an hour, she sat up suddenly in bed.

"Are you planning to leave me, Chester?" she called out in a strangled tone. "Is it your idea to go off with Mrs. Buck?"

But there was no answer. He pretended to be asleep.

Should she let him go? Wouldn't it be easier for all of them, the girls and even Chuck, in the long run? She lay now absolutely still, her wide-open eyes fixed on the blank moon-lit wall of the neighboring house. It was as if her mind had got up and climbed out of her body and had now turned back to contemplate with a sneer its supine former abode. Would *it*, without the encumbrance of that pile of somatic feebleness, have been at the beck and call of the male peacock now suddenly snoring in the next bed? Would she not do better to kick the glittering matrimonial edifice of which she had been so falsely proud into a jumbled pile of smoking masonry? Ah, Justine, Justine! Did not the very violence of her image show that love, soured by humiliation, had already turned to hate? Or was she simply hoping that it had? Did she simply yearn to be liberated from her obsession with this unworthy man?

"Oh, Chester, Chester!" Her lips formed the voiceless appeal. Could he not *see* that he would be nothing without her? And stifling a moan, rolling slowly in her agony from side to side, she bade her mind creep, like a coward, back into its jerry-built home to form a desperate plan.

———

It was not difficult for Justine to find the opportunity to carry out her project. Chester knew all the social engagements of the Bucks and tried to attend as many of these parties as he could. It was at a large dinner given by the Mansfield Gateses that she found her first opportunity, when the gentlemen joined the ladies after coffee and brandy, to get hold of Percy Buck. She had noted with a wry amusement how the little man had tried to escape her down to the end of the long drawing room with its pompous Gallatin portraits. When he turned, however, and saw her upon him, he could only give in and indicate the sofa on which both might comfortably sit.

"I have hunted you down, you see."

"I am most flattered." He seated himself gingerly by her side.

"But you were trying to avoid me, admit it. Oh, I saw you scuttle!" Glancing down the room, she saw that they were safe from interruption. Who, anyway, would want to join Percy Buck?

"Why should I do any such thing?"

"Because you were afraid of what I might want to talk about." She smiled at his gape. "Good heavens, man, you're actually terrified!"

"I don't understand you."

"You're scared to death that I'm going to talk to you about our *cari sposi*. But why on earth shouldn't I?"

"Because we're glad they're such friends?"

"Heavens! Are we?"

"You mean you're not?"

"Not in the least bit! Are you?"

Buck was grave. "I really don't think I can go on with this. Do you consider that a drawing room is the proper place for such a conversation?"

"It's the only place, so far as I'm concerned! Here we are, so to speak, on a stage. As in a French classic drama, where all the action must be kept in the wings. Oh, I don't say we can't indulge in a *tirade* if we like. I probably shall. But it will have to be a *tirade* that fits into a drawing room. You will find, my dear Mr. Buck, that the restraint imposed on us is a necessary condition for thinking. Alone, our emotions might choke us. And you and I *must* think."

He shook his head. "I don't understand you."

"You don't have to understand me. Only listen to me."

"Why should I?"

"Because I want to help you."

"By helping yourself?"

"How else? Look here, Percy Buck. Are you really trying to tell me that you and I aren't in bad trouble?"

He sank back on the sofa, giving up. "All right, all right. Help me."

"What will you do if they go off together?"

His response came in a low growl. "Divorce the whore!"

"Well! You got in your *tirade* first. A short one, but effective. And you kept your voice down. Good. Then here's my second question. What will you do to keep her from going off?"

"You really think they will?"

She considered it. "I think there's enough risk to justify

our having this talk. So I repeat: What will you do to avoid it?"

He collapsed; the small man became a small boy. "Anything!"

"Then there's hope. There may be a way. It's not a conventional way, but the conventional ways never work in our situation. I suggest we offer them their freedom."

"Their freedom! To leave us?"

"Precisely." She spread her hands expansively. "Fling open the doors! We are dealing, you and I, with romantics. Chester is tired of being Lord Chesterfield. He wants to be Lord Byron — before it's too late. He might do any mad thing if it made a big enough scene."

"And Amelie? Does *she* feel that way?"

"Perhaps not quite. But Chester can be very persuasive. Like the Archduke Rudolph, he might lure her to Mayerling."

"You don't mean he'd shoot her!"

Justine repressed a smile. "No. But I mean that any woman has her moments of wanting to kick over the traces. Have you never felt the urge, looking down from a great height, to jump?"

"Never!"

"Neither have I. That's just it. We're the anchors. It's fortunate for such people as Amelie and Chester that we exist. Our job is to strip their fantasy of its glamour. The first thing to remove is its illegality. They must feel free to marry. Free to *have* to marry."

"*Have* to?"

"For Chester, anyway. He must be made to see that it will be his duty to marry Amelie. And why should they go to Europe or Tahiti? Why should she be separated from her child? You and I could arrange to make them an allowance, couldn't we? Maybe you even have a spare house they could live in?"

Percy, still at sea, clutched at a spar. "I have a cottage on the lake at Cazenovia. It belonged to my mother. That's near Syracuse."

"Near Syracuse? Perfect! Why should they not settle in Syracuse — or near Syracuse — and live in a modest fashion? Chester could even write that book on French cathedrals. You know, the one he's always talking about."

"*Is* he always talking about it? How should I know?"

"You shouldn't. Anyway, he'll never write it. And he's going to loathe the woman who tries to make him. Oh, can't you see it? The little house near Syracuse. By the lake, do you say? So isolated and cold in winter. And beautiful Amelie watching him *not* write that book on cathedrals that was going to crown their ardor. And then beautiful Amelie asking him whether he's started it yet. And not quite hearing his answer, so he has to repeat it!"

Buck was still bewildered. "But if they're already in that house, what good does seeing it do *us?* It will be too late!"

"No, because Chester will see it too, and in time for our purposes. He will see it the moment the idea is proposed. He has a vivid imagination. He'll see it, and he won't go!"

"Let me get this straight, Mrs. Bannard. Are you seriously suggesting that I offer my wife her liberty to marry your husband and provide her with a house in Cazenovia and an *income?*"

"I've never been more serious in my life."

"And would you do the same for your husband?"

"Yes. But you must do it first. I'll make *my* offer when Chester tells me of yours. Otherwise, he might smell a plot."

[ 54

"But how can I be sure you'll do it?"

"Do you want me to put it in writing?"

Buck shook his head gravely. "I think I'm going to treat your proposition as an extraordinary joke."

"Think it over."

"May I call you?"

"Any day."

"What a remarkable woman you are!" He gave a deep sigh. "I only wish I'd married one like you."

"But there *aren't* any like me, Mr. Buck!"

"I'm beginning to believe it."

As the Bannards lived only two blocks from the Gateses', they walked home. Chester asked her what she had been talking to Percy Buck about.

"We talked about deafness," she said. "I recommended that his wife get a hearing aid. Then he won't have to shout at her."

———

Two weeks passed in which nothing seemed to happen. Buck did not call, and Chester gave no sign. He seemed unperturbed, but he was a consummate actor — when he chose to be. Justine was on tenterhooks but took care not to show it. Then she and Chester went up to Chelton for the final football game of the season. After Saturday lunch he was closeted alone with the headmaster in his study. Justine, having coffee with the faculty wives in the adjoining parlor, tried not to glance at that closed door. When it finally opened, it revealed a beaming Dr. Stead and a smiling Chester, arm in arm. But he said nothing to her until they had started for the football field. It was a fine clear afternoon, but cold, and she shivered as she walked beside him over the green campus under the great elms.

"Well, if Dr. Stead has his way, I think we're all right. Of course, it's up to the board."

"Oh, Chester!"

"You're still game?"

"Oh, yes! And you?"

"I daresay it wouldn't be altogether a bore."

"Oh, don't be so blasé. You know you're as keen as I am!" She was suddenly afraid that the ecstasy would be too great, that it might rip something inside her. It made her bold. "What about the divine Amelie?"

"What about her?"

"Won't she mind having you so far away?"

He chuckled. "You forget she'll have a house in Lenox."

"It's true! I had forgot!"

"Ah, poor dear Amelie, you needn't worry about her." He strolled ahead a few paces and then turned back to where she had stopped to stare after him. "You've been very patient with me, Justine. You've put up with more than any wife should have to. But I assure you it's all over between me and Mrs. Buck."

"Oh?"

"It's nothing now."

"It's just . . . finished?"

"Finished."

He seemed willing to let it go at this; he strode on again. She hurried after him. "Chester, forgive a woman's curiosity. Was it you that ended it?"

"No, it was she, actually."

"You mean . . . she . . . ceased to care?"

"Oh, I flatter myself it wasn't that. But her husband has

behaved in the most extraordinary fashion. He told her that if she wanted her freedom, she could have it."

"And you said he was such a brute!"

"I misjudged the man. He was actually humble. He even offered her a settlement. I think the poor fellow really loves her, in his own peculiar way. He convinced her so, at least. She said she could never leave him now. Nor do I see how she could."

Justine felt the dry gust in her heart that she had felt in their first serious discussion of the lady. How could she bear that her joy should be so brief? "But if she had said she *would*, would you have gone off with her?"

Chester paused to look up at the sky. "Who knows? We must deal with the present. The past is over, like a bad dream. I came to my senses, thank heaven. Oh, almost at once! As under a cascade of cold water. Think of what I was jeopardizing! You, the children, my friends, my career. And now all this." He embraced the campus with a gesture.

"Ah, yes, all this," she breathed. "You *do* want it, don't you?"

"That's what I discovered, after my scene with Amelie. I don't know when I've been so keen on a thing."

"Well, let us hope that Mrs. Buck has not cost you it," she said in a grimmer tone.

"How could she have done that?"

"People talk, you know!"

"You think there was that much said about us?" he asked in surprise.

"Let us hope not. Come. We don't want to miss the kick-off."

On the following Tuesday morning Justine went downtown to Broad Street to sign her will, an annual event, in the chambers of Danvers & Trevor. When this business had been completed, she went, in response to a note handed to her, to the office of the senior partner, George Cotton. He rose as she appeared in the doorway.

"I knew, of course, that you were coming in, Justine. Notice of the visits of such important clients is always placed on my calendar. I wanted to say hello, but it happens this morning that I have something particular to ask you. Don't worry. It has nothing to do with your legal affairs."

Justine looked away from the long, handsome face before her and glanced about the vast square chamber. She took in the dramatic view of the harbor, the dark prints of urban scenes and the immense mahogany desk, bare of papers, with its heavy, gleaming golden aids to composition.

"I'm always impressed by your office, George. It seems to offer a client such concentrated attention. A very expensive attention, certainly, but complete."

"Well, it's not going to cost you a penny today. Of course, you know I'm chairman of the Chelton Search Committee?"

"And that Chester is a candidate. Of course."

She had long faced the proposition, without bitterness or even regret, that she might have made an error in rejecting, at the age of twenty-two, this man's offer of marriage. There had been a great deal in his favor: he had already, even at that early time, borne on his long, lean, brown face the marks of the dedicated young lawyer whose dedication was going to be recognized. Everyone had spoken of his industry and reliability, and had he not been a law clerk of Justice Holmes? He had not been indifferent, no doubt, to worldly considerations, but her fortune, she had realized even then, had provided only the icing on the cake of his genuine esteem of her. Such a mixture of sense and sensibility was probably preferable to Chester's concealment from himself of the function of her gold in the engine room of his noble vessel of romance. She had turned George down with her eyes wide open to marry a less worthy man because he had *looked* the part that she had suspected even then was partly a role. So were matches made.

"Let me ask you this, Justine. Are you both amenable to the idea?"

"I think we are. It would be a great change in our lives, a challenge. But challenges can be exciting."

"It would be a more restricted life than either of you has been accustomed to. A headmaster lives in a glass house."

"Do you imply, George, that we have something to hide?"

"Not you, Justine. Never. You could live in a crystal vase."

"How cold that sounds!"

George paused. "I'm going to ask you a question that I wouldn't put to any other wife I know, Justine."

"Are you so sure, then, it's a good idea to ask it?"

"No. I'm taking a chance. But I know that you're an unusually objective woman."

"Is that a compliment?"

"From me it is."

"I guess you'd better get on with it, George. What's the question?"

"I can assure you that nobody will ever know that I asked it, or that you answered."

"I see. Unless, of course, *I* tell."

"But you won't."

"Ah! Well, I guess I know what the question is."

"I wonder whether you possibly could." She was silent.

"The appointment of Chester would break the school's tradition of clerical headmasters. We are ready for that. But we should expect a layman to be quite as exemplary in his private life as the strictest cleric. Do you think this expectation would give Chester any trouble?"

"I don't suppose you'd have to count the spoons in the dining hall."

"No. I don't suppose we should."

"Go ahead, George. I'm not going to help you. Put it on the line. What are you afraid of?"

"Very well, I'll be plain. Would Chester have trouble with the younger faculty wives?"

"You mean, would they have trouble with *him?*"

"Either way."

Justine was to remember afterwards that her lack of hesitation had been extraordinary. She had looked into the future and seen it as clearly as if someone had opened before her on that desk a large, vividly illustrated book. To have slammed it shut in front of her mutely gazing friend might have been an act of simple rudeness. "Chester would be on his best behavior for a year, perhaps even two," she heard her own clear tones enunciate. "He would apply himself conscientiously to the job. And he would be a success, too. He would look the part of a great headmaster, and, looking it, for a time he might even a bit be it. But with applause, respect and power — for there is power even in a small academy — would come self-confidence, then pride — and, at last — vanity. A pretty young master's wife would flatter him for her husband's advancement. And she might find herself paying in heavier coin than she had anticipated."

George was too good a lawyer to allow his thunderstruck

reaction to be more than hinted. "Justine, you're wonderful! There's nobody like you!"

"Have I voiced your fears?"

"I'm afraid you have. Your concern for the school — and for Chester — is nothing less than heroic!"

"Unless, deep down, I don't really want to be a head-mistress. If that's what you call a headmaster's wife."

His eyes searched hers. "Ah, but you do!"

She reflected before nodding. "I think I do. But I also think that Chester will be easier to cope with in our present life." She rose; the interview had to be closed. "Good day, George."

He jumped up. "I have always admired you, Justine, but never more than today."

"I doubt that. I think you're rather appalled."

"Stupefied may be a better word. Would you care to lunch with me?"

"No, thanks. Another time. Today, it would be a bit too much. Besides, I have my Book Class."

"And what book do the ladies discuss today?"

"It's our drama session. We do *The Constant Wife*."

"How appropriate!"

"So like a lawyer to beg the question!"

———

The Class met at Adeline Bloodgood's, which it rarely did, as her apartment was small and she had only a single maid. She offered them a chef's salad that was served from a buffet with white wine, and the members relished the atmosphere of a picnic. When the Class adjourned, Justine asked Adeline whether she might stay on to talk to her. Seated by the little fireplace as the maid cleared away, she told her hostess, as succinctly as possible, the story of Mrs. Buck and the Chelton appointment.

Adeline had been a bit tired, for the preparation of the little meal had taken her the whole morning, but as she listened to her friend's tale, her beautiful, faintly worn features became illumined with sympathy. Justine admired her above all the other members. If Adeline was the poorest of them, she was still the most elegant. She bought few clothes, but they were the simplest and best. She affected white silk blouses and black knitted jackets, and she always wore her mother's large pearls tight around her neck to match her prematurely white hair and in contrast to her sapphire eyes. Her skin, a rather patchy brown, made those eyes wonderfully glow. Adeline had beauty, Justine acknowledged, but it was the beauty of a virgin priestess.

"I certainly recognize my 'detached' Justine in what you tell me," Adeline reflected, some moments after her friend had finished. "I see it all, and so vividly! All, that is, that you put to me. And should you have really liked to go to Chelton?"

"I think it would have been amusing."

"Then you are of a discipline! I suppose there is no chance of your going now?"

"Hardly."

"Well — you have done your duty. I hope, my dear, that it will prove a consolation."

"Ah, but that's it, Adeline. *Was* I doing my duty? Or was I simply punishing Chester?"

"Punishing him? For flirting with Mrs. Buck?"

"For fooling me into thinking that he took as a tragedy what I had taken as a farce. And now taking as a farce what *I* take as a tragedy!"

"But he gave the lady up! What more can a consort ask?"

"Ah, but *why* did he give her up? Because she wouldn't go. And because he couldn't even be bothered to persuade her. Because he was entranced with the prospect of a shiny new toy. The school!"

"All that may be perfectly true. But he returned to the path of virtue. Any motive for *that* must be a good one."

"That's where you Catholics have the advantage over us. We're chained to our motives. *They* must be proper!"

"I haven't lived a life with Protestants to know nothing of their motives. But why was not your motive in keeping Chelton School and Chester Bannard apart a proper one? You saw the school's need and your husband's weakness, and you decided they had better go their separate ways."

"True. But why was I so sure that Chester had not reached an age when he might be less liable to these diversions? Was I not playing God?"

"We do that every time we take any action involving another human being."

"But surely, knowing that I was in the grip of resentment, I should have thought very carefully before embarking on a course of action that might be revenge on Chester for making an ass of me?"

"You did think, my dear. And most carefully, too. I am sure that Chester will be happier without the danger of scandal that his particular vulnerability might expose him to in a small New England community. And I wonder whether the school will not be better off with a less lively head. So who has lost out but yourself? Surely *that* should square the worst Protestant conscience!"

"Ah, don't underestimate that conscience! You're leaving

out of consideration the satisfaction I may have got in thwarting Chester. Satisfaction in my revenge for his having made me so wretched over an affair that meant so little to him!"

Adeline threw up her hands. "Of course, I'm an old maid and don't know about these things. But isn't thwarting one's spouse one of the harmless pleasures that you girls marry for?"

"But there was no love in my heart when I did it — that's the difference!"

"No love? Oh, come, Justine, you can't convince me of that."

"The embers of love, maybe."

"But you're full of love, my dear! Chester must have his share of it."

"What makes you so sure that I'm full of love?"

"I can vouch for your love of Chuck, anyway!"

"What credit do I get for loving a son?"

"Is credit what you want? There speaks the tycoon's granddaughter!"

Justine rose abruptly, as if she had got what she sought — or at least what she deserved. "*Now*, do you see, Adeline, why we all come to you for judgment?"

# 6

I SHOULD BE WILLING to wager that there will be some readers of this little volume who will not have noticed that the preceding chapter was written from the hypothesized point of view of Justine Bannard. E. M. Forster believed that the question of the point of view from which any tale is told is of much greater interest to writers than to readers, that few of the latter bother to distinguish between action viewed by a single character, or by many characters, or by an "omniscient author." Heresy to the shade of the great Henry James!

I resorted to the method of fiction (and of the single point of view) to relate what I suppose to have happened in a critical year of Justine's life, because, dig as I would, I could never seem to unearth all of the facts. There was only so much that I could get out of her son, Chuck, and as for Justine herself, she was a woman of great reserve — except when she had a specific need of candor. Most of the Book Class resembled her in this; it is one of the distinguishing marks between their generation and mine. My contemporaries generally have very little discretion. On a recent flight to

Europe the lady in the adjoining seat to mine cut through the usual preliminaries between strangers to announce right off that her husband was impotent!

With Georgia Bristed, however, I shall have no need to resort to fictional methods. I can rely on my own direct observations. Anything else, indeed, might not be fair, for she was the one member of the Book Class that I think, in retrospect, I did not really like. I must therefore lean over backwards to avoid prejudice.

Georgia in 1950 looked as she was to look for two decades afterwards and as she had looked for two decades before: a tall, gaunt, rangy woman with a brown face, messy gray-black hair and small, sharp, glowing blue eyes. When she sat down and rested her chin on clasped hands over a triangle of long brown arms and blinked at you, it was hard to imagine that she was not as humane as she was shrewd. But was she? She was certainly forceful; she might have been an excellent headmistress, or even a drill sergeant, had fate not chosen her to keep a salon. But this description leaves out her most extraordinary characteristic, her equanimity; nothing ever seemed to ruffle her or cause her to lose her temper. Indeed, I sometimes wondered whether she had a temper to lose. And may not a person lacking a temper lack other things as well?

Her husband, Jo, known to old and young as "Pop," was a big, plain, oafish man with a great bray of a laugh who would, with his freely tendered platitudes, have constituted a kind of clown for his wife's group, had not a grudging respect for the fortune that he had unaccountably gained as an odd-lots broker and the memory of his rare but terrible bursts of temper moderated their scorn. It always intrigued me that Pop seemed to have no conception of his intellectual disqualifications for the role of salon host. He adored the discussions of Georgia's circle, to which he infrequently, albeit noisily, contributed, and was perfectly content to play the solicitous bartender, filling glasses and pulling up chairs. I admired his simplicity, particularly for the way it played up the affectations so rampant in such gatherings, and he and I, a kind of Mutt and Jeff, were frequently to be seen chatting together in a corner over a game of backgammon, in flagrant violation of the rules of organized discussion. Georgia would glance at us in mild reproval, but she knew when to leave her unpredictable spouse alone.

In Georgia the hostess seemed to have largely consumed the woman. Like a busy spider, she was constantly engaged in spinning her web of plans to catch new recruits. Henry James, in one of his ghost stories, created the character of a British peer whose magnificent public presence simply evaporated when he was not on view, so that if a mischievous observer were to peek into his chamber when this nobleman fancied himself alone, he would find it empty. So, when the last guest had departed, when Pop had stumbled to bed and sunk into slumber, when the maids had finally "turned out," the lady of the house may have suffered a temporary eclipse.

When she first established her salon, in the nineteen thirties, she and Pop purchased a large red brick house of the Federal period in West Tenth Street, just off Fifth Avenue, and furnished it in the same era: gilt-framed mirrors crowned with eagles, chairs and commodes resting on claws or hoofs, horsehair sofas and primitive paintings, all of the kind that could then be picked up for next to nothing and are worth a fortune today. Georgia had estimated that if on Tenth Street she could strike a mean between the Village to the south and fashion to the north, she might mix artists and writers with bankers and politicians to the edification of both, and to a considerable extent she had succeeded. It was perfectly possible, in 1935, at Bristed soirées, to meet E. E. Cummings, Walter Lippmann, Rosa Ponselle and Thomas Lamont.

But by the time I started going to them, in the late nineteen forties, it was already evident that the great Georgia was losing ground. It was not that people didn't come; too many did. Haunted by the American notion that to cease to grow is to dwindle, she had started to proliferate her invitations, asking people to bring people, so that at times one wondered whether there were any common denominator in her reception rooms but drinks and noise. Our hostess, I soon discovered, was aware of this imperfection.

"It's a mess, isn't it?" she said to me one night, gazing pensively about the room. "I've got to cut back."

"Or cut it out."

"Is it really that bad?" She showed not the least resentment at my freedom. "I don't think I have to be quite that drastic. What would you say to my trying it with a smaller group — more *choisi* — and for a different day, perhaps Wednesdays? Could I count on you, Chris? Till I get it going?"

"Yours in the ranks of death!"

Mother was amused by my intimacy with her old friend. "Watch out, she'll gobble you up!" she warned me. Georgia had always been ready to make use of any human being that she found to hand, regardless of age or sex. I recalled, in my Yale days, a subscription dance at the Plaza where she had been a patroness, and where her daughter Gladys had been badly "stuck." The moment she saw me approach the receiving line, she took me aside to offer me two tickets to a hit show the next day if I would look after the poor girl for an hour. It was like a bargain between two schoolboys, to be clinched with a wink and a handshake. I had promptly agreed.

And now she and I seemed to be joined in the rejuvenation of her salon! On Wednesday nights a group of some twenty or more would forgather at nine and with wine and whiskey, under candlelight, discuss current political questions. For it was in that direction that Georgia was setting her course.

I had no objection to the direction — I took as keen an interest in current events as any of them — but I did not relish the rising star of Rufus Wilberding, a tall, middle-aged bachelor, of vast means and supercilious manners, as Georgia's obvious candidate for the leader of our debates. If she was the chairman of the board, Wilberding was evidently slated to be our executive director.

"Why do we have to put up with that tory?" I asked her crossly one night when Wilberding had held forth, fatiguingly, on communists in the State Department.

"Don't you like Rufus?"

"Do *you?* Does anyone?"

It struck me that Georgia's hesitation indicated not so much a doubt as a sense of the irrelevance of my question.

"Of course I like him. Consider all he's done with his money for museums and libraries. People are beginning to call him 'Mr. New York.' "

"What people? The ones he's bought? Has he bought you, Georgia?"

"He didn't have to. I came for nothing."

"You hold yourself so cheap?"

"Darling, I'm a raddled old whore! Didn't you know?"

69 ]

"My education about the sacred Book Class never ceases."

"Oh, the Book Class — how you go on about it. We'll have to make you a member."

"It's been my life's ambition! But shouldn't I have to go to Scandinavia for a sex change?"

"It won't be necessary. Just slip into an old tea gown." Here she laughed her strong, oddly uncatty laugh. "But I want you to like Rufus. I want you both to help me with this salon. You've noticed how I'm changing its make-up?"

I stared. "You mean it's a deliberate process?"

"Oh, perfectly."

"You've lined them all up and barked, 'Right face!'"

She clapped her hands. "Squads right! Or is it right by squadrons?" I supposed this was some dim recollection from 1917, when she had accompanied Pop to the military training camp at Plattsburgh. "That's where the future is, you see. In the nineteen twenties it was the thing to be bohemian. In the thirties you had to be left or at least liberal. In the forties we were all for war and victory, and in the fifties it will be . . ."

"Fascism?"

"Say, conservatism," she corrected me, still without offense. "We're going to learn to appreciate things native. The American way will be the keynote."

"Does that mean your drawing room will be full of rednecks?"

"Ah, my dear, that shows your vulgar prejudice. It has long been a tenet of the left that they have a monopoly on the artists and intellectuals. But it's not so. Shakespeare was a political conservative."

"And so was Wagner," I sneered. "We all know *The Ring* shows the undermining of the state by Jews. Are you doing this from personal conviction, Georgia, or because you think it's the fashion?"

When she again hesitated, I wondered whether she saw any difference between the two. "Let me be frank with you, Chris. You're a very intelligent young man. I am fifty-eight years old."

"Sixty, dear. I know my Book Class."

"What a bastard you are! All right, sixty. It makes my point all the stronger. How many *good* years do I have left? Years when I have the proper zest to entertain? Pop's pushing seventy. Who knows when we may have to move to Florida or some ghastly place? I've lost my appeal to youth. My last top parties were in the thirties, when you could mix right and left in politics, in the arts, in everything. Well, now that's out. Now one must choose. I'm too old to go left, and besides, there are limits even to Pop's patience. So where does that leave me?"

I raised my hand in a Nazi salute. "*Sieg heil!*"

"You find one real Nazi in my house, and I'll give you a hundred bucks!"

"Ah, but we'd never agree on the definition. However, Georgia, don't worry. I shan't desert you. I shall continue to be one of your 'faithful,' as Madame Verdurin would put it. It will be great sport, anyway, to see if you can pull it off."

"Voyeur!" she retorted.

Rufus Wilberding, as I made it out, represented a new kind of power seeker on the urban scene; he sought power, through inherited wealth, over cultural institutions. The boards of these had been made up in the past of business executives whose ambition had been sufficiently satisfied in the downtown world of profit and who were willing to allow the administration of their charities to be handled by curators who carefully flattered them. But the curators had little chance to flatter and less to fool Wilberding. His cold, green stare was all-embracing, and a gesture of his thin alabaster hand was final. Rufus laughed a good deal; he even liked to affect a pose of effeteness as he sprawled his long, lank figure over a chair and rested his handsome head against its back to look at you quizzically, but underneath he was always ready, suspicious, alert. And in right-wing politics he had found at last his faith.

As I studied each new recruit for our Wednesday nights, I found that all had the same ticket of entry: a morbid fear of the Soviet Union and the infiltration of its doctrine. Sometimes this barely showed itself behind the affable manners of well-bred, statistic-citing lawyers and their dowdy wives; sometimes it was expressed by the writers and journalists among us in cutting but unimpassioned disparagement of every public figure; sometimes it was draped in theological terms, usually by Catholic converts; sometimes it was more candidly offered in ostensibly joking accusations of treason against persons of hitherto unimpeachable citizenship. But always it was cool and temperless, as if the one thing that brought these people together was a conviction that they were fighting a battle that was almost lost and that their only hope lay in a sustained presence of mind. But why, I wondered, did they always search for the low motive in even nonpolitical matters? Why if a newspaper reported a rape, did they smirk and insinuate that the victim had invited it?

Rufus was standing before the fire one night with a kittenish look in his eyes, and I suspected that he was waiting for the right moment to spring a lively piece of news on us.

"We have another indictment," he announced at last.

"Oh, Rufus, what?"

"Another Hiss?"

"Very like, very like. I have it from an Assistant United States Attorney. It will be out tomorrow. Another 'fine young man with good connections,' an Eli, of all things, who has sold his immortal soul to traffic with the enemy."

"Who, Rufus?"

"Did you say he was a Yale man?" I demanded. "What year?"

"Oh, about your time, I should think, Chris. You may have known him. Our hostess knows his mother, who was once her father's secretary. His name is Calvin Townsend."

"Cal Townsend!" I was surprised at how shocked I was. I had not seen him since before the war. But his name lit an immediate glow in my heart. "What has *he* done?"

"You do know him?"

"I knew him, anyway. But what's he done, damn it all, Rufus?"

"He is accused of delivering classified documents to a Russian agent while he was employed by the Department of Commerce in nineteen forty-one. What can you tell us about him, Chris?"

"Very little. I haven't seen him in years."

"But was he known to be leftist at Yale?"

I shrugged. "A bit so, I guess. A lot of people were."

"So there you are!"

"There *you* are, Rufus," I retorted tartly. "Leave me out of it, please. Why would a Russian agent care about papers in the Commerce Department? I'll wait till it's proved."

I was too upset now to want to say any more about it, and I took Pop into the conservatory for the game of backgammon that he was always glad to play. At an early hour I went home.

I could not get to sleep for a couple of hours that night, thinking of Calvin Townsend. I saw that grave, handsome, frowning face under the steely blond curls; I saw the taut, tight figure under the cheap, well-fitting suit, so constantly worn yet so invariably pressed. There must have been vanity behind that puritan exterior to keep a modest wardrobe so consistently presentable. Cal was a bursary student; he worked in a restaurant at odd hours and never left the campus, as most of my group did, for parties and weekends. He had not attended a New England "prep" school, and his social circle rarely intersected with ours, but his mother, as secretary to Mrs. Bristed's famous old medical father, had acquired friends among his fashionable patients, and her friends' sons had been enjoined by their mothers to look up Cal. Their overtures, however, had been largely snubbed, and only I, intrigued by his *farouche* manner and reputation for radical politics, had persisted to a mild breakthrough. Cal is one of the few people in my life I have allowed to "tolerate" me.

He was much too proud to let me treat him to meals or shows, but I was a clever tempter, and I took him one night to the opening of a Clifford Odets play in New Haven. He was excited by it — at least as excited as he ever permitted himself to show — and afterwards, in a scrupulous demonstration of gratitude, he insisted on buying me a beer. I was able to persuade him to allow me to counter his offer with several others, and we became almost confidential in the corner of our shabby bar.

"What will there be for me to do in your brave new world?" I asked him. "For, mind you, I absolutely decline to drive a tractor."

"You know our motto: From each according to his ability,

to each according to his need." Here Cal actually chuckled. "But I doubt that any society could provide all the things *you* seem to need."

"Will there be no writers and artists, then, in Utopia?"

"Ultimately, yes. But there'll be a lot of work to do first. I'll tell you what we *won't* need, and that is bankers."

"But I'm not going to be a banker! That's for my brother, Manny. The last thing Father wants in Wall Street is *me*. In England the younger sons could go into the church or the army, but no one does that here. I fear I must resign myself to being a poet."

"What about lending a hand to the underdog, Chris?" Cal's clear skin was lit up now with an earnestness that I found flattering. He was capable of brief moments of charm. "You strike me as better than the rest of your crowd. Oh, I know, you like to pose as a dude and a dandy, but I suspect you've got some kind of social conscience. Don't kid yourself, though. It won't survive forever in the world you live in. The disease of piggery is too catching."

"You think we're all pigs?"

"If you're not, you will be. Look at your fathers. You've told me about yours."

I rather regretted, now, that in an effort to convince him that our boats were not entirely dissimilar, I had tossed Father out of mine. Cal had the irritating leftist trick of remembering every concession that you made and never making any himself. "But everybody's father's not like mine. Look at Chuck Bannard's. He's an architect. He embellishes the world."

Cal snorted in derision. "With copies of European palaces! Emblems of an outmoded class system that was even more putrid than the one we've got! At least your old man's a pirate and makes no bones about it. He's the kind of enemy a man can respect. But spare me Mr. Bannard."

"What about our mothers, then? You can't lump mine with Father, any more than you can lump Mrs. Bannard with Mr. Bannard."

"Why can't I?"

"Well, to begin with, don't they have what you call a social conscience? They take a very active interest in charities."

"Do you really expect me to buy that shit?"

I began to be angry. "Why not? They support all kinds of good works."

"Those women are completely manipulated by their husbands."

"That shows how little you know them!"

"Oh, I know they're bossy in the home and spend a lot of the money. Sure. The men toss them that in return for the real power. The minute something important was at stake, look how your ma knuckled under! Show me one woman in that crowd who knows how to vote her stock in a proxy fight. Show me one, for that matter, who knows a stock from a bond!"

"You forget that many of them are far richer than their husbands. Mrs. Bannard, for example."

"I'll concede *she* may not be controlled by her husband. But *cherchez l'homme*. She's controlled by the man downtown who handles her money."

"Stocks and bonds aren't the only way to exert influence. Mother and her friends are a real force for good in our society."

"In sassiety, maybe," he sneered, and I reflected that Cal was much less attractive when he sneered. "But they're too

[ 76

tainted to do any real good in the world. The system has corrupted them."

"Now you're being absurd."

"I'm perfectly serious. You don't know what those women are really like until you've worked for them. Until you've seen them from the other side — the side of the menials who wait on them. You should hear the tales *my* mother has to tell. In her job she had to deal with their servants. She learned about the multitudes of poor Irish women who slave for your ma and her likes, living in tiny cubicles on the unheated top floors of their mansions, working around the clock with one day off and no place to go, and never allowed to have a man visit them. No chance to marry, no chance to earn a pension, nothing to look forward to but to go back to Ireland in their decrepitude and be murdered by starving relatives for the few pennies they've saved!"

"The last I doubt."

"It actually happened to a maid of Mrs. Jessup's. Mother told me!"

"But even if the system is bad — and I admit it's not ideal — Mother and her friends didn't start it."

"No, but they're the beneficiaries! They're corrupted in the same way Southern women were corrupted by having slaves."

I was beginning to weary of the argument. "Of course everybody's happy as clams in the Soviet Union," I retorted.

This sample of our conversation will explain why, although I was drawn to Cal, we never became close friends. He wasn't interested in any companionship that was divorced from social causes, and he soon saw that I was never going to be a recruit. He probably found my emphasis on the importance of human relationships bourgeois. After graduation I lost sight of him. I heard that he had gone into government, in the Department of Commerce, and that he later served, with some distinction, in the marine corps in the Pacific. He was reputed to have become disillusioned with the Soviet Union, and certainly his employment after the war by a large chemical company in Chicago did not have a radical sound. I sent him Christmas cards, but he never responded. I had not even known that he had been transferred to New York and that he had married a pretty girl of no known communist affiliations.

Chuck Bannard, my Yale roommate, had been the only member of my college group who had seen anything of Cal. I took him aside to discuss the indictment before the members' night dinner at the Patroons Club. Chuck, at thirty, suggested more the approach of middle age than the retreat of youth. The rough-and-tumble youngster had become a rather sleek investment banker; the muscle was still there, under the perfectly fitting dinner jacket, but it might soon enough be fat. His smile had some of the old boyish charm, but it was rarer. Chuck, alas, was surer of himself; his doubts had formed a principal asset.

"I was sorry to hear about it, of course, Chris. One doesn't like to see a classmate indicted. But, frankly, I never cared for Townsend. He was always such a surly bastard. I put up with him only because you liked him."

"I don't think liking him or not liking him is the question now. Isn't it whether or not we ought to help him?"

"How?"

"By offering to contribute to the expenses of his defense."

"Can't he afford a lawyer?"

"I doubt it. His company's already fired him. How much

money can a man have saved at our age? We know there was no family dough."

"Well, don't you think his former associates should pay for him?"

"You mean the guys that fired him?"

"Of course not. I mean the reds he worked for."

"You assume then he's guilty?"

"I hear there's no doubt about it. You remember Tim Horan? He's in the U.S. Attorney's Office. He told me it was an open-and-shut case."

"You believe that Cal gave classified documents to communist agents?"

"And then lied about it."

"But what secrets could the Commerce Department have had that Russia wanted?"

"I don't say that Russia wanted them. I say he gave them. The fact that the papers were classified is enough for me."

"But suppose Cal believed that Russia was the only country in the world that still believed in peace? That was a possibility then. Suppose he had some statistics or something — I don't know what — that he thought would help Russia persuade the belligerents to confer?"

"It still wasn't his business to declassify documents."

"Of course it wasn't! But doesn't it affect the degree of his crime? Isn't there a difference between assisting a neutral nation to mediate, and handing over nuclear secrets to a hostile one?"

"Perhaps. But if that were the case, why didn't Cal tell the truth? Why didn't he make a clean breast of the whole thing?"

"Because nobody would believe him in the hysterical atmosphere we're living in!"

"Is *that* your criterion? That we tell the truth only in nonhysterical times? I can remember when you had higher standards."

He had me there, of course. He remembered my attitude in Father's trial. But it still seemed to me that it was easy enough for Chuck to be high-minded, sitting there with his pale, chilled Martini, his fragrant cigar, his round, red-cheeked countenance.

I went down to the Federal District Court on Foley Square the next day to attend a session of Cal's trial. A former communist agent, one Thomas Squire, was on the stand all morning, under heavy cross-examination by Cal's blustering and formidable attorney, the famous Max Eagers. Squire was a small, feral creature with watery eyes who needed a shave, but he remained stubbornly calm, seemingly almost unconcerned, under the pounding breakers of Eagers' angry and tenacious interrogation. He clung to his story, a persistently floating spar in those churning waters, that he had received the documents known as "Exhibits 3, 4 and 5" from the defendant in a Washington cafeteria. I began to be afraid that he was telling the truth.

I kept glancing at Cal, whose seat was only a few yards from mine. He followed the testimony intently, but without any expression of disgust or alarm. Occasionally he would whisper something in the ear of a young lawyer, a clerk of the great Eagers, who sat beside him. Time and treason had not diminished his good looks; he faced a hostile world with the same appealing truculence that he had presented to a potentially unfriendly one.

At the first recess, when I went out to the lobby for a cigarette, I noted that Cal and Mr. Eagers were also stretching their legs. When my eyes met those of my old classmate, he gave no sign of recognition. Nonetheless I went over boldly to him and held out my hand.

"Here's wishing you all the luck in the world, Cal."

He took my hand and held it for a moment, looking at me gravely. Then he let it suddenly drop. "What really brings you here, Gates? Is it our festival of trials? First Hiss, then the communist leaders, and now me? A Roman holiday?"

"For that crack to an old friend you deserve to be embarrassed. I came to see if you didn't need a hand with the expenses of your defense." Here I made a little bow to Eagers, who gazed at me with astonishment. "You are being represented brilliantly — that I have seen. But no doubt also expensively."

Cal's features were seized by something almost like disappointment. Why? Did he *want* to hate us all? Then he grabbed my hand again. "You're a great little guy, Chris. You were always the one good apple in a rotten crowd. But thank's a million. Millard Gross is picking up the tab."

We heard the cry that the court was reconvening, and Cal and his counsel turned away from me. I decided that I would not go back to my seat. To tell the truth, I had been disgusted by the mention of Gross' name. He was a rich, aging playboy and a notorious fellow traveler.

I was tempted never to go back to the Bristed salon, but curiosity as to what the sensitive ears of Georgia's "faithful" might have picked up about the case led me to break my resolution the very next Wednesday, and nine o'clock found me once again at West Tenth Street. It was a snowy night, and a small group, no more than a dozen, sat cozily around a fire. Georgia, who was holding a bunch of letters in her lap, explained that they had an intimate connection with the Townsend affair.

"Townsend's mother used to work for my father, you know. She's an absolute old darling. Of course, this business about her son has almost killed her. When I went to call on her yesterday, I found her in a pitiable state. She insisted that I take home these letters that her son had written her when he was at Yale. She says they will prove what a patriotic American he is. Of course, it goes without saying that she's totally convinced of his innocence."

"He hasn't been found guilty yet," I reminded her.

"It's hard for Christopher to believe that a fellow Eli, an old blue, could betray king and country," came the chuckling tones of Rufus Wilberding. "I envy Yale the loyalties she inspires. We poor Harvard men are only too inclined to find reds under each other's beds."

"I only said he hadn't been convicted," I pointed out icily.

"And I'm sure Benedict Arnold graduated from a perfectly respectable academy," Georgia intervened impatiently. "I have no intention of arguing either side of the Townsend case. I simply thought that some of you might be interested to hear the letters."

There was an immediate chorus of agreement. "But have we the right to hear them?" I demanded sternly. "Did Mrs. Townsend know that she was offering bread and circuses to this mob?"

"But, my dear Christopher, why else do you suppose the poor woman gave me the letters?" Georgia protested. "She wants me to publish them far and wide! She maintains that they exculpate her son entirely. Which is why I propose that Rufus, who reads aloud so well, should do us the honors tonight. Of course, it's always possible that we may adjudge them differently from the way a doting parent does. She takes her chance."

There was nothing more that I could say, but the reading of those letters was wormwood to me. I was at first tempted to walk out, but curiosity held me fast. I wanted to know what Cal had been writing at such length to his mother at a time when I had found it difficult to elicit anything like that number of words from him in conversation. Why was it so much more amusing to write to a dull old woman who worked for Mrs. Bristed's fashionable quack of a father than discuss life and art with one of the luminaries of his Yale class?

Wilberding's reading voice, so touted by our hostess, was in fact tiresomely affected and smug. He seemed to be picking up poor Cal's youthful phrases with a pair of silver tongs to hold them disdainfully before our presumably mocking eyes. He smiled with a feigned tolerance for juvenile enthusiasms; he chuckled with a feigned amusement at boyish idealism. He was as superior to it all as a cardinal of the Inquisition, and he would have shrugged his shoulders just as carelessly had he seen his victim hauled off to the stake.

And the letters themselves? Cal had poured out his heart in indignation at every instance of social injustice that he had read in the newspapers: strike-breaking, lockouts, union-busting, lynchings. I was beginning a bit to wonder why his mother thought this agitated reporting such conclusive evidence of his patriotism, when Wilberding came to a letter describing F.D.R. as the great American of the century. This provoked the urbane interpreter of the epistles into his first overt expression of disgust.

83 ]

"You can see the rot starting here," he observed parenthetically, peering down at us over his spectacles. "It's a striking instance of how the virus attacks a young mind."

"You mean because he had the bad taste to admire his President?" I asked.

"In Spain, Chris, you may recall, it was the Loyalists who were the reds."

I exploded. "When I think of the letters *I* was writing to *my* mother at that time! All about debutante parties and shows and where to go in the summer! While Cal was telling his about the agony of America! And you call that rot? What do you think was happening to *me?*"

"You were experiencing what I should call a normal adolescence."

"Because I wasn't thinking? Are you afraid to have young people think?"

I got up in disgust and asked Pop abruptly to come and play a game of backgammon with me in the next room. "Go on with the damn letters," I threw over my shoulder to Rufus. "I just don't want to hear them, that's all."

In the dining room I poured myself a stiff drink of brandy from the decanter on the sideboard. Then, sitting down with Pop at the backgammon table, I asked him with belated compunction whether he minded missing the reading.

"Not at all," he replied in his high cheerful tone. "I'd much rather play with you, my boy. And we can always read the letters in the papers."

"You mean that Townsend's mother is planning to publish them?"

"No, but Georgia has had mimeographed copies made. Rufus is going to give them to the U.S. Attorney."

I stared. "For use in the trial?"

"Yes. To show the early red affiliation, don't you know." Pop pronounced this as one word: "dontcherno."

"No, I don't know!"

"Well, Georgia and Rufus seem to regard it as their public duty."

"To betray a mother's confidence?"

"But she *did* tell Georgia she wanted the letters read, didn't she?"

I studied that long, innocent, gaping, mottled countenance. "She wanted them read, presumably by people who might befriend her son. Not by his prosecutors!"

"Oh. You think it's wrong, eh?"

"I think it's damnable!"

"Look here, young fellow, that's pretty strong. You're speaking of my wife."

"I am not! I'm speaking of Rufus Wilberding, who has put her up to this. And I'll be even franker with you. I consider it your plain duty to save Georgia from the infamy of being hornswoggled by that self-righteous pisspot into betraying an old woman's confidence. There! Now throw me out of the house if you want to."

Pop was ominously still. "My duty, eh?" he repeated grimly. "You're telling me my duty, Gates?"

"I am! And what's more, I think you ought to thank me for it!" There was a tense silence. But I knew from the way that he bit his lip that he was weakening. "Only you can save her!"

Bristed began to turn it over. "You think I should just march in there and seize those letters?"

"*And* the mimeographs."

"And return them to Mrs. Townsend?"

"I'm counting on you, Pop. Wilberding is laughing up his

sleeve at you. He doesn't think you'd dare!" Something flashed into my memory: I grabbed it, reckless. "Someone asked him the other day about the 'famous Mrs. Bristed.' The person wanted to know whether her husband was still alive. Do you know what Wilberding's reply was?"

Pop really gaped now. "What?"

"He said, 'Technically.' "

I now followed my furious host to the door of the drawing room and watched with delight as he shouted: "See here, Georgia, I want those letters! And the mimeographs, too. Every one of them! They were given us in trust, and they're going to be returned in trust. I'll take them myself to Mrs. Townsend. Tomorrow morning!"

It was like Georgia that even this outburst did not seem to anger her. She glanced around the chamber with a deprecating smile. "Decidedly, I am not having much success with my letters tonight. First Chris and now Jo." She rose to gather them up from the table by which Wilberding had been speaking. "Here they are, my dear," she continued, handing them to her husband. "I appreciate your returning them for me." She then addressed the others. "And now may I suggest a complete change of subject. Who here has read the Hazlip report on Taiwan?"

I do not accuse Georgia of keeping copies of Cal's letters to his mother and forwarding them to the U.S. Attorney, but somebody, no doubt Wilberding, managed it, and when I next attended a session of his trial, I had the mortification of hearing them read a second time. Never shall I forget the look that Cal cast at his stricken old mother. It bore — at least so it seemed to me — no hint of anger at his betrayal, only a compassion for what the poor woman must be suffering at the humiliation of having allowed these documents, by whatever means, to escape from her possession. I think at that moment that I actually hated Georgia Bristed!

I cannot believe, however, in retrospect, that these letters had much effect on judge or jury. There was plenty of damning evidence without them. Poor Cal was convicted and sentenced to five years in prison. When I tried to speak to him in court after the verdict, he turned abruptly away from me. His wife told me afterwards that he had learned from his mother that she had shown the letters to Mrs. Bristed, and he must have at once connected her with me.

I had intended someday, somehow, to break through Cal's wall, his own as well as the prison's, to explain to him about the letters. But the opportunity was denied me, for he was murdered in prison during an inmates' riot. It seems likely that he had been the victim of a homosexual whose advances he had spurned.

For a long time I could hardly bear to think of his end. When I awoke in the night from nightmares about it, I would leap from my bed and do setting-up exercises feverishly to try to drive the horror from my mind. It seemed to me that the society in which I lived was like a troop of ballet dancers hopping gently on a tender crust of earth. One step too heavily taken would plunge us into a cesspool of snapping submarine creatures. On top was the world — what world? The world of the Book Class? — and below there was hell. Cal had chosen hell, and where did that leave me?

I was able for some years to salve my conscience with the trifle of supporting his widow, but her happy second marriage to a prosperous accountant has deprived me of even that.

Needless to say, I went no more to Georgia Bristed's salon,

which became even more sordidly rightist in the ensuing McCarthy reign of terror. I heard about it, but not directly, for very few of my friends, or even of Mother's, were sympathetic with the witch hunters. This may come as a surprise to younger readers, who tend to assume that everyone living through that era had to be a fascist, a martyr or a silent coward, but it is nonetheless true that at any really fashionable New York dinner party of the time, the bravest thing a person could do was to praise Joe McCarthy. And this brings me to a final note of justice (if that be the word) to Georgia Bristed.

It was shortly after the Senate vote of censure that initiated the downfall of the demagogue, when, finding myself seated one night by Georgia at a dinner of Justine Bannard's, I indulged in a small whinny of triumph.

"Do you weep for your great man?" I asked her.

"Why should I care what happens to him?" she retorted. "McCarthy was always a drunk and a windbag. It's high time we were rid of him."

"So now you throw him to the dogs?" I was almost shocked.

"He was never a hero of mine."

"Well, can you deny that your parlor has been a hothouse of his supporters?"

"He's been supported in my house, it is true. I will even admit that he's given us some fun. But enough is enough, Chris. I have become weary of hearing his name. And then people keep making the same old arguments, over and over!"

I found myself half-stifled with outrage. But articulation soon returned. "Do you realize, Georgia, that reputations have been blasted, lives ruined and the whole country turned into a bath of hate by that man's willful lies? And to you he's nothing but a subject of chatter for a soirée?"

Then at last, at long last, the lady proved not only that she had a temper but that she could lose it.

"There ought to be *some* limit to the spatter that we poor females have to take from your asinine male sports! First it's cowboys and Indians, then cops and robbers; now it's reds and patriots. One side has a heavenly time dressing up as martyrs, while the other struts about, draped in the Stars and Stripes. Everyone knows it's just a game — name one sane person who's afraid of a communist revolution! If I'd wanted to be popular, I'd have taken the anti-McCarthy side long ago. It was obvious from the beginning that he was too hollow to last, that he was being kept alive only by the press. But every hostess in town was against him — what choice had I but to take the other tack? So that fashionable liberal conformists like yourself, who turn to *The New York Times* editorial page every morning for your marching orders, can sneer at my one pathetic little gesture of independence!"

I was so staggered by her argument that for a moment I could think of nothing to say. Then I realized there was no point in saying anything.

"Go left, Georgia!" I exclaimed with a sneer. "Better red than dead."

"You don't think it's too late?"

# 7

ADELINE BLOODGOOD, the oldest member of the Book Class, the most beautiful and its sole virgin, lived in a tiny apartment in the East Seventies amid a clutter of associational knickknacks and a few good things. Over the mantel, as on an altar, was a charcoal sketch by Sargent of the late Judge Luke Melrose, bald, hook-nosed, with half-closed but critically staring eyes, whose paid companion and housekeeper she had been until his death in 1930. "Uncle Luke," though not related to her, had been the great thing in Adeline's life. She was the priestess who tended his shrine, and it was to her that students of the great jurist's life and works directed their respectful steps.

I had always admired her striking looks — the snow-white hair, the sapphire eyes, the brown skin, the perfectly molded features — and I reveled in her high, clear, precise articulation. Adeline made a little event of each idea in even a casual dialogue. She was in constant quest of the beautiful, in language, in friendship, in books, in the daily routine. She did not waste a scrap of life, which made my visits to her at teatime oases in an urban existence where the very streets seemed gray with the litter of lost opportunities.

She was a popular member of the Book Class, but I noted shades of condescension. She had missed what most of them regarded as a woman's purpose in life — a fruitful union with a male — and they tended to view her concern with forms and appearances as a somewhat pathetic substitute for a more valid fulfillment. Mother was probably the worst offender in this respect; she went so far as to find my pleasure in Adeline's company a trifle ridiculous.

"I don't see what she has to offer a young man," she insisted.

"She simply offers him a sense of life! Most people are as good as dead fifty minutes out of every hour."

"Oh, Chris, how can you say that an old maid knows anything about life? Isn't it just what she hasn't had?"

"Adeline, in my opinion, has lived more than any of your friends."

"Now you're trying to get my goat."

"I'm perfectly serious! You all think life consists of tolerating the lovemaking of some clumsy ape and bearing his brats."

"Your father, I'm sure, would appreciate that way of putting it!"

"But isn't it true? Adeline can find meaning and beauty in things to which the rest of you are utterly blind. In the horizon at the end of a city street. In a slant of morning light. Even in the feet of fellow passengers in a streetcar!"

Mother sniffed, and I had a vision that contrasted her with Adeline: the solid Roman matron and the Greek Tanagra figure. "That's all just pose. And while we're on the subject,

I think I ought to point out that a young man who's always hanging around a precious old maid invites people not to take him seriously. Manny was speaking about that just the other day. He said that you . . ."

"I don't give a hot damn what Manny thinks!" I interrupted her wrathfully. "Or rather what he says, for I know he can't think. I happen to be extremely choosy about who my friends are, and I went out of my way to make one of Adeline. Manny, of course, couldn't see any use for a woman except in a way too vulgar for me to express to you."

Mother at this time — I was thirty-two — was beginning to be a bit fearsome when I lost my temper. Father was showing his age, and she depended more on my company and love. I spied a flicker of concession in her lowered eyes.

"Well, is it a *crime* that I'd rather have you spend your time with some nice girl who might one day be my daughter-in-law?" she protested.

So there it was again, the eternal hope! Mother could never surrender the image, however chimerical, of her baby boy as a bridegroom. And this obsession with the altar was shared by all of the Book Class. The generation before them had been known to keep children, particularly daughters, in wedless servitude, but even the most possessive parent in the Class would have thrown down the drawbridge to let in a spouse.

"You sound like a desperate Jewish mama," I retorted. " 'Anybody gotta nice girl for my Christy?' You ought to know by now that I don't go along with your idea that life is an ark into which the dumb animals must be made to march in pairs."

"I only want you to be happy, dear."

"And I will be happy! I *am* happy. As happy as Manny,

anyway, with that querulous little wife of his." Mother was silent at this. I knew that she did not like my sister-in-law, but torture would not have extracted the avowal from her. "Try not to worry about me, Ma. Try to believe there may be more kinds of the good life than those that happen to appeal to you."

"You're never going to convince me that Adeline's is one!"

But I had a special object in cultivating the society of Adeline Bloodgood, and one that Mother would have regarded as perfectly respectable, had I not been too disgusted by her narrow views to enlighten her. I was a lifelong admirer of the writings of Adeline's late employer and patron, Luke Melrose, and I hoped to put together a piece about him, with Adeline's help. This was the "literary" phase of my career, when, in addition to decorating, I had produced a slender volume of poems, another of essays and two short novels.

Melrose had been a judge on the New York Court of Appeals for thirty years, but his reputation was as great among laymen as at the bar. He had gained in 1910 a nation-wide fame with the publication of *Equity*, a book that has always been the despair of librarians. Does it belong on the shelf of history or law or philosophy, or even autobiography? The author starts out with the dusty subject of remedial justice in the ancient courts of chancery, but before his reader is through, he has been taken on a kind of romp through history and the cogitating existence of Luke Melrose. It is almost impossible to describe the work except as a unique aesthetic experience.

I had attended law school for a pleasant year at the beautiful University of Virginia, never with the serious intention of practicing, or even of graduating, but simply to postpone the decision of a career and to keep Father off my back. I never developed much affection for the law and what to me were its barbarous tautologies, but the language of Luke Melrose, the "Walter Pater of jurisprudence," had been a blessed discovery. He was the one asset that I bore away from my Charlottesville interlude, besides the happy memory of the red earth and the serpentine walls and white columns of Mr. Jefferson's "lawn." To this day I keep *The Notable Opinions of Luke Melrose* by my bedside, each page marked with my interlineations. I open it now at random to find:

> Chalcedon was called the city of the blind, because its founders rejected the nobler site of Byzantium, lying at their feet.

Did I say Pater? It's Gibbon!

Melrose sustained me through dreary law school courses. I sensed him behind the murky grays and blacks of our dismal industrial world, beaming the golden arc of his judicial flashlight into the muddy corners of grade-crossing collisions, falling cranes, exploding gas tanks, matrimonial hatred, corporate greed, taxes evaded or ruthlessly imposed and all the contemptible sewage of modern litigation. I fancied a kind of brief redemption from the hopeless vulgarity of it all in the glory of his prose. Like myself, he had loathed statistics and statutes; his art found all the justice that it needed in mystic communion with the common law.

I guess I have made clear why I raked the ashes of Adeline's flame for nuggets from that source. She was delighted at the idea that I might write something about "Uncle Luke," but reluctant to set pen to paper herself.

"I see it all so clearly in my mind's eye," she told me one afternoon at teatime. "I feel I should spoil it if I tried to set it down."

"But the world is always hungry for more about Melrose."

"Why do you suppose they care so much?" she mused, looking up at the Sargent charcoal sketch. "I mean the people who don't even read him. And who wouldn't understand him if they did."

"Because they like to simplify their cultural lives, and nothing does this better than picking one great man to represent each field. For example, science can be lumped under Einstein. And music under Toscanini."

"And art under Picasso?"

"You get the idea exactly. And law, of course, under Melrose. What I want to suggest is that you and I talk about your life with him for, say, an hour, every couple of weeks. I should then write up what you say, type it out and give it to you to read. If you don't like it, we'd just quit, that's all."

Adeline became deeply contemplative. "What is it exactly that you would be looking for?"

"I don't know. I'd have to see what comes out. What can we lose?"

"I'm not sure. Perhaps everything."

"Oh, we can stop before that! Give it a try, anyway."

"When would you want to start?"

"This very minute! For an experiment, anyway. Now just relax, and I'll ask you a question. If you don't want to answer it, don't."

"All right." She was apprehensive, but clearly intrigued. She closed her eyes and placed her hands on the arms of her chair. "Go ahead."

"When did you first go to live with Judge Melrose?"

"In nineteen twenty. My family had known his, in Buffalo, for many years. I had always admired and liked him, and he treated me as a particular favorite among the younger gen-

eration. When his wife died, his nieces had to find someone
to keep house for him." Adeline opened her eyes now to
gaze up at the sketch. Apparently, it did not reproach her,
for her voice, when she continued, was freer. "He was then
already in his seventies. He had no children. And, of course,
a mind like his could have nothing to do with the pots and
pans of housekeeping. Besides, he was frail and very small.
And I was thirty-four and, as the nieces no doubt saw it,
hopelessly single and hard up. Oh, of course, I jumped at
the chance! They didn't risk much, either. Even if Uncle
Luke had become senile and taken it into his head to marry
me, the money was all in trust."

She stopped abruptly with a look of dismay. "You see, my
dear, the kind of thing that pops out. I don't think I want
to go on with this."

"Why shouldn't it pop out? Any niece who places a
beautiful woman in the home of an old uncle has to face the
possibility that he may marry her. I'm sure they talked it out
thoroughly."

"But it's so vulgar!" Adeline's head shake conveyed real
distress. "Everything becomes vulgar when broken into
details. Even people thinking that Uncle Luke dominated
me, kept me from marrying!"

"*Did* they think that?"

"My own mother did! But it's not true! He was the
kindest, the dearest man that ever breathed."

"Well, isn't that just what people should be told?"

This seemed to surprise her. "I suppose it is."

"And who should tell them but you?"

At last I had made an impression. "I'll have to think it
out. But I couldn't do any more today. I simply couldn't!"

"I'm not asking you to."

[ 96

A week later, when I telephoned her, she agreed hesitantly to try again. When she asked what my first question would be, so that she could be thinking of her answer before our meeting, my eye happened to fall on the little volume that I kept by my bed.

"The editor of *The Notable Opinions of Luke Melrose* is a man called Nicholas Reynolds. Did you know him?"

"Know him?" Her high tone trilled with surprise. "My dear boy, he once asked me to marry him!"

"Well, tell me about *that*, then."

"And not about Uncle Luke?"

"Oh, I have a feeling he'll come into it."

"That's just the trouble!"

But she agreed at last to see me the following day at five, and all the time I was there, I listened in absolute silence. I knew enough about interviewing to be aware how easily people not used to public life can be put off by note-taking or recording machines. If one writes up one's notes immediately afterwards, it is possible to catch nearly all of any interview. Here is what I transcribed that night.

# 8

How shall I begin? Well, let me tell you about Uncle
Luke's house. It was a typical Manhattan brownstone, in
East Thirty-third Street, except that it was filled to the brim
with books. Space was made here and there on the walls for
a few fine prints — Whistlers, Dürers, even a Rembrandt —
and some Japanese screens. There must have been feminine
things in Mrs. Melrose's day, but the library, like a jungle,
had swallowed them up. Uncle Luke divided his time between this narrow, sober dwelling and a shingle cottage in
Narragansett. When his court was sitting, we occupied a
suite in an Albany hotel.

We were constantly together, and people came to treat us
socially as a couple. Sometimes his nieces thought that I
"presumed" too much and tried to put me "in my place,"
whatever that was, but Uncle Luke could get very angry
indeed if he suspected that anyone was snubbing me, so
their hostility had to be covert. It may help to explain to you
why our relationship was so accepted, even in the stiffest
social circles, when I add that not only were there four

decades between our ages, there were six inches between our heights! Uncle Luke barely came up to my shoulder.

As you can see in Sargent's drawing, he was what is called a dapper man, abrupt and forceful in his manner, with piercing eyes, a sharp aquiline nose and a high bald dome. He could be imperious, and he was impatient of blunderers, but there was kindness beneath this gruffness and shyness behind his bluster. And he was basically the humblest of men. He used to explain his cases to me, making the facts as simple as possible, and sometimes he would ask me how I should decide one. When I protested that I was not qualified, he would shrug and mutter: "Shucks, you know more than half the men on my court. More, really, because you haven't the limitations of the legal mind. You can still make out the forest, even if you like the trees!"

He made a point of questioning everything that other people took for granted, and he hated to be taken for granted himself. There was what I used to call a thespian side of his nature that made him enjoy acting out the reverse of any popular expectation that he might have aroused. This was particularly true with unimaginative admirers. I remember a young male caller who quoted a Harvard classmate of the Judge's, one Sol Feigin, a great accumulator, as having said, "Luke Melrose has had the career the rest of us only dreamed of as undergraduates!" Uncle Luke raised his eyebrows, pursed his lips and then seemed almost to expectorate his cutting reply: "Did old Sol say that? Did he indeed? Did he utter that banal compliment as he strode up and down his great art gallery, under his Goyas and Velásquezes, sinking knee-deep in carpet? Well, go back to old Sol, young man, and tell him I'd give all my precious opinions for just one of his chinking millions!"

99 ]

And he told a reporter who asked him, on his seventy-fifth birthday, what was the secret of a happy old age, "A good game of bridge, which, tragically, I have never learned to play."

But, for all his habit of rebuffing naïve admirers, he was eager to communicate with younger people. I know that he envied Justice Holmes the disciples who flocked to the little house on "Eye" Street in Washington. The trouble was that whereas Holmes' opinions excited the admiration of young men who were keen on building a better society, Uncle Luke's jewels of percipience in the common law appealed to more aesthetic types, and he was inclined to be tart with aesthetic males.

Nicholas Reynolds was much more the first than the second type, and I think that Uncle Luke would have taken to him right away, had I not made a mess of their first meeting.

Uncle Luke did not like to go out in society, and he preferred to have me stay home with him, but he had a conscience about my social life and was always talking about my wasting my "youth" cooped up with an old man. So he would send me out, as he put it, a dove from the ark, and to bring him back, incidentally, news of the great world. He showed a surprising interest, for so deep a thinker, in gossip from Gotham. I suppose a lawyer, like a novelist, can be nourished by almost any tidbits from the human banquet.

It was at a dinner party in Manhattan given by Georgia and Pop Bristed that I met Nick, who came nearer than anyone else to being the "man in my life." He was then about forty, perhaps four years older than I, a professor of law at Columbia, and had already gained a considerable reputation with a treatise on the legislative processes of the different states, called *The American Law Maker*. Of course, you haven't heard of it — law books quickly date — but I was pleased to discover that he was a great admirer of Uncle Luke's. I didn't know until much later that he had requested our hostess to put me next to him, knowing of my position in the Judge's household.

Let me describe Nick. He was dark complexioned, and what is called "burly"; he had thick, black hair and bushy eyebrows. Some people thought he was too shaggy, but he was a forceful talker and made a good deal of being direct, or "honest," as he always put it. He was, as Uncle Luke once said, almost too manly to be a man.

I remember that we had two wines at dinner, which was not common in Prohibition days, and our conversation touched on the subject of the Eighteenth Amendment. I told him that Uncle Luke, who was a great oenologist, had much resented its passage, and even went so far as to consider it unconstitutional.

"But how can a part of the Constitution be unconstitutional?" he asked.

"Well, if two articles are in conflict, doesn't one of them have to be unconstitutional?"

"And which article is in conflict with the Eighteenth Amendment?"

"Doesn't the preamble speak of securing the blessings of liberty? Uncle Luke considers fine wine just such a blessing."

"I see! The Judge is a wit as well as a seer. But in all seriousness, Miss Bloodgood, I suspect him of harboring no great enthusiasm for constitutions. Like statutes, they are the work of legislators. Judge Melrose is a common law man. And who declares the common law? The judges! Every time a statute is passed, their rule is eroded. And one doesn't have to look very far into the future to spy a world where a judge's power will be confined to the mere construction of statutes."

"And what of Uncle Luke's beautiful opinions?" I asked in dismay. "Will they not always be read?"

"By students, of course. But their practical use will have largely disappeared."

"How very sad!"

"It is history. He will have been a part of it. He will have played a great role. That is all any of us can ask."

I found that I did not like this. It was very important to me that Uncle Luke's opinions should always be read, not just as curiosities of a legal past, odd little bits of glass gleaming in the dust heap of forgotten jurisprudence, but as an integral, glowing part of the golden column of words that supported the very structure of Anglo-Saxon civilization.

"Mightn't he be preserved in some kind of history or biography?" I inquired.

"Or better yet, in a book of samples of his writings. It could be a work of literature as well as law. You see, I've thought it all out."

"Oh, Mr. Reynolds!" I clasped my hands together. "Would *you* put together such a book?"

As he looked at me, very intently now, I think I began to realize that we were going to be good friends.

"We might do it together!" he exclaimed.

"Would you like to meet Uncle Luke?"

"Can you ask?"

I decided to introduce him only as a friend of mine and let him take his own steps in presenting his project to the Judge. This, it turned out, was a mistake. Uncle Luke was inclined to be a bit sour with my callers; in his own house he liked the attention to be centered on himself.

How I see them together at that first meeting! Uncle Luke, sitting in his low chair by the fire, his bald head gleaming in its light, touching his fingertips together, his eyes settled coolly on his visitor — or victim. And Nick, all rumbling, fumbling attention, leaning so far forward as to seem about to tumble over and crush his diminutive host.

The conversation was desultory, and I began to be uneasy. Would Uncle Luke prove a disillusionment to my new friend? How could I make my lion roar? Desperately, I introduced the subject of Italian Renaissance art, in which Uncle Luke took a keen interest.

"Have you heard from BB lately?" I inquired of him.

Uncle Luke maintained a correspondence with Bernard Berenson, at whose villa in Fiesole he had made several holiday visits.

"As a matter of fact, I had a letter this morning. BB, it seems, has a bone to pick with me about my letters."

"And what could that bone be?" I asked, still rather artificially, smiling at Nick in order to bring him into a dialogue from which Uncle Luke seemed bent on excluding him.

"He complains of my too-graceful closings. He points out that through the years I have always signed myself in hyperbolic fashion, as 'your devoted pupil' or 'your admiring apprentice,' or 'your constant disciple.' "

"And what is wrong with that?"

"He wants to know why I never subscribe myself just 'affectionately.' "

I think it may have been a small resentment of Uncle Luke's continued ignoring of Nick that kept me from asking the obviously anticipated question. But Nick did it for me.

"Well, Judge? Why don't you?"

"Because I don't *like* him!"

Uncle Luke barked out the words in a way that made me fear that Nick might take them as applied to himself. But he didn't; his delighted laugh was almost a roar.

"What a superb summation of a long friendship! Is he really the old swindler they say?"

If Uncle Luke, however, permitted himself considerable latitude with the reputation of his friends, he allowed no such freedom to his housekeeper's acquaintance.

"I see no reason to impugn Mr. Berenson's honor," he retorted stiffly. "It's not his fault if some inane Yankee collector is willing to pay an extra ten grand for a Vigée-Lebrun that *he* authenticates."

"But doesn't the price of the authentication go up with the attribution?"

"I don't follow you, sir."

"Ten thousand may be what the collector pays to be convinced that his purchase is a Vigée-Lebrun. But what if he wants it to be a Rembrandt? What will that cost? A hundred thousand?"

Uncle Luke stared at such boldness. "The painters to whom you refer are well over a century apart. You could hardly expect even an inane Yankee to be *that* confused."

"Or Mr. Berenson to be that unscrupulous?"

"The idea is absurd," Uncle Luke snapped, concluding the discussion.

When poor Nick had gone, I allowed myself for the first time to be openly critical of Uncle Luke.

"I do not see why you have to be quite so abrupt with a gentleman whose only offense is that he admires you above any lawyer living or dead!"

"My dear girl, I had no idea he did!" he exclaimed, with evident distress. "I gave him credit for taking a proper view of *you*, to be sure, but it never crossed my mind that *I* was anything but an old guardian bear whose cave he had to penetrate."

"On the contrary, I was nothing but an excuse! He wants to put together an anthology of your prose. And I thought it was such a beautiful idea! Now I daresay he'll never come back."

"Oh, let us not take such a somber view," Uncle Luke riposted, rubbing his hands together briskly. "I doubt that any irreparable harm has been done. Invite the delightful young man here again. We might even send him an autographed copy of *Equity*. What do you think, child?"

Of course, Nick was only too glad to come back, and a friendship now rapidly sprang up between the two. Uncle Luke was enchanted by the idea of the anthology, and he and I gave up our reading aloud of evenings to pore over his old opinions, searching for the finest phrases. Of course, many of these were buried in cases that I could not readily understand, but he would supply me with the basic facts of each in a summation of masterly clarity — his memory was prodigious. It was like looking for wildflowers in a grand shadowy forest. How I loved it! I seemed at last to be an actual part of his compositions.

What was a good deal less satisfactory was the triangular relationship that developed between Uncle Luke, Nick and myself. Uncle Luke had started with the assumption that Nick, like so many of the younger men who came to pay him tribute, would be totally uncritical of the object revered. But this, alas, was far from the case. Nick, in fact, was nothing if not disputatious; he found it difficult to believe that his brave, pulsating, at times almost obstreperous humanitarianism could fail to strike a kindred spark in any heart that he admired. Just as Uncle Luke assumed the younger man to be his blind disciple in the worship of the common law, so did the latter take too easily for granted that the great Judge would be happy to ameliorate the rigors of that law's application in any case where humanity cried out.

For example, in a discussion involving the right of a district attorney to use evidence against a defendant obtained in an unlawful search, Nick was very much distressed to find Uncle Luke firmly on the side of the police.

"But, sir," he protested, "mustn't we balance the social needs? Our need to be protected from unlawful search with our need to be protected from criminals?"

"Our? *I* have no need to be protected from unlawful search! There are no bloodstained weapons on *my* premises! And, anyway, the wronged householder has his right of action against the intruding bailiff."

"Much good that will do him when he's hanged!"

I could see that Uncle Luke did not like this, and I shook my head warningly at Nick, who rose rather abruptly to take his leave. Out in the hall, before he departed, he permitted himself a rather sharp comment: "I'm afraid the old boy's a bit of a fanatic about his common law. If he had to choose between it and the human race in a marine disaster, I can guess which I'd find in the lifeboat!"

"Doesn't detachment become a judge?"

"But there are limits, Adeline!"

"And I'm sure Uncle Luke hasn't exceeded them. He may get a bit carried away by an argument, but his heart is always warm."

"How could it not be when one such as yours beats so close?"

"Why, Nick! You're being gallant!"

"Will you walk as far as the avenue with me?"

"No! Goodbye!"

But the smile with which I closed the door upon him was far from discouraging. I had become, as they say, "interested" in Nicholas Reynolds.

I had been sufficiently upset by even this minor disagreement between the two men to beg Uncle Luke to excuse me from their next conference. But to my surprise he demurred.

"I like to have you there, Adeline. It helps you to understand the kind of mind that fellow has. Oh, he's bright and enthusiastic enough — I don't take that from him. But he's emotional. His edges are blurred. I'm afraid that his is not an intellect of the first rank."

"But, darling Uncle Luke, what difference does it make what kind of mind *I* think he has?"

"Because he admires you. Anyone can see that. And when a young man who's not exactly ugly takes that much interest in a beautiful young woman — well, things can happen."

"But Nick and I aren't that young. And nothing's going to happen!"

"Are you sure of that, Adeline?" He was suddenly grave.

"Of course I'm sure!" I had been brought up in a family where it was considered good taste to deny such things. Nobody dreamed that it involved deception.

"You relieve me. Because he's not good enough for you."

I didn't like this at all, but after what I'd said, I couldn't complain. "Oh, a man doesn't have to be very good to be good enough for me. But, Uncle Luke, you're dreaming. I'm thirty-six. I'm an old maid!"

He was apparently satisfied by my disclaimer, for nothing further was said of Nick. But he still would not allow me to abstain from the conferences. He seemed determined that

I should learn at first hand what was and what was not a first-class legal mind. Alas, my lessons were not to last much longer, for our sessions blew up in a horrid row.

Oh, that terrible day when we discussed the legal defense of insanity! Nick had been much upset by Uncle Luke's dissent in the notorious *Snade* case, where the majority of his brethren had spared the life of a killer who had slit the throat of his infant son, as Abraham had been prepared to do to Isaac's, at the imagined command of his deity.

"But the poor creature was mad as a hatter, Judge!" Nick exclaimed when the three of us were seated in the library after a Sunday lunch. "I could hardly believe it when I saw you'd dissented."

"The defendant knew his son. He recognized the boy's mortality. And he decided to suppress it. If that is not murder most foul, I do not know what is. At common law he'd have been lucky to be hanged. More probably he'd have been burned alive."

"But we're not living in the reign of Henry the Eighth! The man was a crazy fanatic!"

"If a man allows himself to become so involved in religious thinking that he imagines himself the direct recipient of divine instructions — which always in these cases seem to be orders to slaughter fellow humans — that is his choice. He need not have so involved himself."

"Do you not recognize compulsions, sir? Snade could not help himself. He *had* to carry out the imagined mandate!"

"And having carried it out, he should pay the penalty."

"Is that the great Judge Melrose speaking?" Nick was greatly exercised. "Could you really bear to see that poor idiot strapped into that grim chair and filled with volts?"

"The method of execution is hardly relevant," Uncle Luke replied icily. "Unless you are proceeding to an argument against capital punishment in general. I am simply saying that Snade was guilty of murder in the first degree. My function is not concerned with penalties; it ends with definition. But I might add, speaking nonjudicially, that I fail to comprehend the logic that requires our society to keep alive the Jehovah-obeying Mr. Snade while it puts to death, as it did only last year, the unfortunate Mr. Childs, who, to save his sorely harassed wife, rid the globe of a peculiarly fiendish black-mailer!"

"Am I to take it, sir, that you would use the criminal law as a means of disposing of mental defectives?"

"Certainly not! I simply advert to a consequence of such laws being carried out that does not cause me to shed tears." Here Uncle Luke suddenly turned to me. "Would *you* weep for Mr. Snade, Adeline, if, after slitting a little boy's throat in the fullest awareness of what he was doing, he was painlessly removed from the possibility of ever doing so again?"

I should have realized how important this appeal to me was. I should, at any cost, not have made Uncle Luke seem doubly abandoned. But it suddenly struck me that, at least in this case, Nick was on the side of the angels, and I could not, even for Uncle Luke, come down on the side of the terrible chair that I had seen photographed in an evening paper, square and bare, with straps and thongs, a kind of horrible robot reaching out arms to embrace its victim.

"Oh, no, Uncle Luke, I can't bear to think of it. Indeed, I *should* weep for Mr. Snade! Can you conceive of the hell that poor creature has been put through? To kill his own child! And to believe so passionately in a god who would order it! And then to suffer death for what, by his dim lights, he believed he had to do. Oh, no, such a man must be in torment. Why should we do anything but weep for him?"

Uncle Luke became very white as I spoke; his lips were pursed to a small red ball. "You two must really excuse me. I shall not inflict my callous presence on your bleeding hearts!"

"Uncle Luke!" I gasped. "Please!"

But he had risen to leave the room, one arm violently gesturing that he was not to be followed.

Nick turned to me with a mighty shrug. "Well, I guess that's the end of *The Notable Opinions of Luke Melrose*."

I burst into tears. "Oh, Nick, don't say it! Uncle Luke will get over this. I know he will."

"But *I* won't. I see him now. And I don't like what I see."

I cannot tell you how agonizing their decision was to me. I saw in it the looming-up for me of a choice that I seemed to have dreaded all my life. For was it not the choice between form and substance, and placed in such a way as to make any selection of form seem arid and sterile? Oh, I could see how people would hoot at me! Did I put words over deeds, manners over heart, an old man over a young one? But it wasn't fair! I knew there was a great heart behind Uncle Luke's beautiful conception of law, and I suspected the existence of a considerable ego behind Nick's affection for the common man. My mother, who had met Nick and liked him, had warned me that I shouldn't sacrifice myself to be a vestal virgin, but I freely confess that this concept was not unattractive to me. In our century, the carnal world is too widely considered the only one. You don't agree, Christopher? Oh, I see. You simply smile.

Anyway, Uncle Luke went to his club that night for

dinner, and the next morning, when we met at breakfast, he did not so much as refer to our little scene or to Nick. I could not imagine that he would not ultimately speak of one or the other, but he never did. He had an immense capacity for putting distasteful memories aside. I never even knew whether he felt ashamed of himself for his brief show of temper. He completely eliminated Nick from his speech, if not from his mind. It was only some years after his death that Nick completed and finally published the little volume that you tell me, Christopher, you keep by your bed.

Nick must have told my mother of the quarrel, for she gave me a straight piece of her mind. Mother was the kind of handsome, stern Yankee woman of the last century whom one could easily imagine passing ammunition to a husband in a stockade besieged by Indians and even taking the rifle, if need be, from his lifeless hand to continue resistance to the end. On her visits from Buffalo, she acted as if nothing that happened in so decadent a metropolis as New York could surprise her.

"I'll tell you what I think, Adeline, and then I'll hold my tongue. Mr. Reynolds is a good man, and I think he wants to marry you. If you turn him away because you cannot love him, you will be doing the right thing. I have no patience with people who think that a woman should marry at any cost. But if you turn him away because he doesn't get on with the Judge, then I call you a fool."

"Oh, Mother, I don't know *what* I feel!" I cried and burst into tears.

"Then don't make an irrevocable decision before you do," she warned me in her dry tone. "Luke Melrose isn't going to live forever, but he'll probably live until you're too old to be asked again."

At breakfast on the morning that Uncle Luke and I were to take the train for Albany, he gazed at me gravely across the table, as he always did to preface a serious topic.

"Are you quite sure, my dear, that you wish to come? That you wouldn't rather stay in New York for the next two weeks? I think I can manage without you."

"Uncle Luke, don't you *want* me?"

"More than anything in the world, child. But old men must learn not to be selfish. You have your life to lead. I occupy too much of it as it is."

"Never! So long as you want me, I want to be with you!"

"You are sure?"

"Absolutely."

"Then I have everything my heart could want."

If you knew, Christopher, how those words touched me! It was very difficult for Uncle Luke to articulate his personal feelings; he was almost morbidly shy. But that his feelings were deep I had never doubted, and to learn now that my silly self occupied such a niche in his heart gave me a kind of ecstasy, even though it was in conflict with what I had begun to feel for Nick.

"Maybe then, dear child, this is the appropriate moment for me to impart to you a piece of information. It is not important information, for it deals with a subject that to all civilized minds must be forever unimportant: money. But that is all the more reason to get it over with. I have established a small trust for you."

"Oh, Uncle Luke! No!"

He held up a hand to check any further outburst. "It is not any great thing. Most of what I live on is itself in trust. But it should keep you decently if you are frugal. And the great point is this: it is yours, all yours. You can leave me tomorrow. You can marry tomorrow. There is no way I can get it back or that you can give it back. You are free, my dear. Absolutely free. That is the only way I want you."

"Ah, but, Uncle Luke, if with one hand you cast me away, with another you grapple me to your side!"

"Do you imply that I wish to hold you with gratitude? It is not so. The little trust, in my opinion, is no more than what you have already earned. Your choice is a free one. If you will not see it that way, you have not the free mind you should have — after all my teaching. Don't disappoint me, child. Don't be mawkish."

"I'll try!" I cried in anguish. His adjective made my cheeks burn!

I did not hear from Nick during the first week of our Albany session, but one morning, when Uncle Luke was on the bench, the hotel desk rang up to say that Mr. Reynolds was in the lobby, and I went hastily down to meet him. I could see at once that he was very agitated. He had come, he blurted right out, to ask me to marry him! Right away, here, in Albany! He seemed of the opinion that I was being held somehow against my will, that I had to be rescued, as from a dungeon. He could not have pleaded his case more ineptly.

What my mother, I am sure, never believed to her dying day was that the choice I made on that cold winter morning, sitting on the little iron chair by the potted palm, with bell-boys hurrying to and fro, was made by a mind that knew itself. I saw before me a good, a worthy man, and one to whom I was indeed attracted, but there was something almost weak in the tempestuousness of his need for me, something verging on the melodramatic in his vision of my predicament. It suddenly seemed to me that he was offering just the life that I had always suspected I had *not* been shaped for: the life of tumult, of passion, the life, if you will, of the flesh. But he did not make it enticing. He made it seem . . . well, rather blustering. There was something about Nick that seemed to protest too much that *he* was life and that *I* was lifelessness, and that life was superior, that life was the only thing! Uncle Luke, in contrast, seemed as high and serene as a mountain over a teeming jungle.

What really happened that morning, Christopher, was that I found that I couldn't accept second-best. I knew that Uncle Luke was not going to live forever — only, perhaps, as Mother had suggested, just long enough to abandon me at an age when there would be no further likelihood of a second proposal — but I did not care. I had found my mission, and I was satisfied.

When Uncle Luke came home for lunch that day and asked me whether I had had an eventful morning, I replied that it had been significantly noneventful. I then told him that I had declined a proposal of marriage. He did not ask me from whom I had received it. He reflected in silence for several minutes.

"Would your mother approve?"

"I fear not."

"Well, I will not insult you by asking you whether you know your own mind."

"Uncle Luke, I'll never leave you!"

———

The foregoing I wrote out on the night after Adeline told me her story. I had it typed and then reworked it carefully until it seemed to me that I could actually hear her talking.

I will admit that I was rather proud of it and looked forward to her favorable reaction. I gave it to her doorman with a note that I should call the next day to discuss it. But when I arrived as stipulated, a single glance told me that my brave experiment had been a failure.

"Oh, Chris, I can *never* go on with it!"

"Why?" I exclaimed, almost indignantly. "Is it so bad?"

"No, it's so good. I mean *I'm* so bad. You've got it so right. Oh, with a vengeance!"

"A vengeance? You mean a vengeance against *him?*"

"Against Uncle Luke? Well, no, vengeance isn't the right word. Because, poor darling, he never did me a wrong!"

I was so disgusted by this that I redoomed my already doomed project. "He simply gobbled you up, hook, line and sinker!"

"Oh, that's what people say, I know," she wailed, wringing her hands in distress. "That's what my mother always said. I've learned to accept that. There's no way of convincing people of the contrary. But the terrible thing about your brilliant piece, darling Chris, is that now I see that *I* said it, too!"

"Said that the Judge was selfish and possessive?"

"Yes! That he was a monster!"

I stared at her hard. "And he wasn't?"

"Never! He was the dearest of the dear. And what you have so fiendishly — ah, no, not you, for it is *I* who am the fiend — dredged up from the murky depths of what I suppose Dr. Freud would call my *id* is the deeply buried resentment of a horrid child who must blame her surrogate father for everything!"

I thought this over in silence. What could I say? To agree

with her would be to confirm her intolerable sense of guilt, and to deny it would be to sully the image of the old man that had formed the light of her life.

"Let us say that *I* was the fiend," I compromised. "That the little interview is not a work of journalism. That it is fiction, pure and simple." But I still could not resist a burst of pride. "Even a work of art!"

"Oh, no, it's true, too true," she moaned.

"Yes, but true of what? Of me, not you."

She looked at me searchingly. "You mean that you . . ."

"Thought he was a monster. And determined to make him one. I put it all in. Do you want me to go over the piece, line by line, and show you how I did it?"

"No!" She thrust the paper back in my hands. "I want to believe you! I don't ever want to read the thing again. Or even talk about it. And now I suggest you mix us one of your very very dryest Martinis!"

# 9

THE MOST PATHETIC — or perhaps I should say the only pathetic — member of the Book Class was Leila Lee. She called herself "Mrs. Lee," although that was her maiden name. She had been twice married and twice divorced, from George Washburn and from Tony Meiksel; the second had been such a horror that she could not endure to bear his label, and it would have seemed quixotic to resume that of his discarded predecessor. But, logical as her choice may have been, it nonetheless made her stand out in undesirable isolation in a group of women to whom the retention of a born name by a matron smacked vulgarly of greasepaint and footlights.

Leila's name, however, was not the cause of her being seen by them as "different." *She* saw herself as different in that she was more feminine, and she could never fathom why the Class did not agree that this made her enviable. But they didn't. They liked her, but she was always, nonetheless, "poor Leila" to them.

What I am really talking about, of course, is sex appeal, or, more accurately, the attitude of the Book Class towards it. To Leila, who had been a beauty in a day when a great deal was made of beauty, when simply being beautiful was considered an adequate occupation, the great business of life was men. What she could never take in was not that her friends in the Class had other businesses, but that they refused to concede that hers was even a respectable one. Leila knew that women the world over were constantly concerned with men; she read it in romantic novels, she saw it in romantic movies and plays; she discussed it happily with hairdressers, nail-polishers, dressmakers and shop girls, and had not her husbands and lovers confirmed it? How was it that this dowdy — yes, dowdy! — group, which met to discuss novels about great passions that they could have known only in print dared to dub her (as she was sure they all mentally did) a tart?

I did not become a friend of Leila's until she was in her late sixties, in 1957, when I started playing bridge one night a week at Blodgett's, a card club. She and I were occasional partners. Of course, I had known her since my childhood, but I had tended to think of her as a charming pinhead, much less interesting than Mother's other friends. I was impressed now by the quality of her game. Of course, there were no idiots at Blodgett's; the stakes were too high. And she was still stunning to look at, tall, fine, stylish in black and gold, with large jewelry, big pins shaped like bees, and heavy gold bracelets that clinked together as she deftly dealt, incessantly smoking a cigarette in a long jade holder. The lovely looks were, it is true, by this time a bit frozen, and the golden-pink hair was, of course, dyed, but there was still an air of extraordinary grace and refinement in the soft gray eyes, the delicate aquiline nose, the high, clear forehead, the long lineless cheeks with the beauty spots. If Leila was trying to look like a flapper of the Texas Guinan epoch, she never quite succeeded in shedding the lady innate in her. Her breeding showed itself in her every gesture and particularly in the entrancing softness of her tone, mixed though it was with occasional huskiness.

She liked to pretend at Blodgett's that she and I were refugees from a strange world that none of the other "regulars" would understand.

"Oh, Christopher's a mere baby," she would tell them at our table. "He could be my son, of course. But, still, he's been to strange places with me. Like Toumai, in the Kipling story. We've seen the elephants dance, haven't we, honey?"

She had at last given up men for cards, a wise transition. She lived in a tiny jewel of a flat in an expensive apartment hotel, into which she had squeezed all the best things of a much more spacious past, a curious mishmash of Art Deco and Louis XV, so that I was always afraid of using a Tiffany vase for an ash tray or placing a dirty sole on an Aubusson. Her friends, mostly women now and vaguely demimonde, were all card players, but she rigorously preserved her one link with her old life and never missed a session of the Book Class. "It has always been my tie with respectability," she rather boasted.

Her family, the Lees, according to my mother, had been the kind of old New Yorkers who had always been "in society," without ever having done anything distinguished or even without having very much money. They were gentle gentlefolk, good-tempered and well turned-out, extreme only in their conventionality. But Leila's beauty had knocked their tradition out of equilibrium: it had tempted them to try for something more, and she had, with much encouragement, "captured" George Washburn, as dull as he was rich, in a "marriage of reason," which, as Henry James put it, is more apt to be a marriage of madness. Childless and bored, she had ultimately left Washburn, but his discovery of her diary had reduced her settlement to a fraction of what she had regarded as her due, yet not so small a one as to keep her from being herself the victim of a matrimonial adventurer in the person of Tony Meiksel. After her second divorce there had been other men but no further husbands, and she had begun to drink. By the time she and I became friends this had gone so far that any proposed partner of hers at Blodgett's found himself well advised to look at her carefully before they sat down.

One evening, when I had a sniff of her breath, I said very firmly: "Leila, you're tired tonight. I suggest that cards are hardly what the doctor ordered. Let me take you home."

She obeyed meekly enough, but in the lobby of her building, which was only a block from Blodgett's, she suggested that I come up for a drink.

"Do you really think *that's* what you need?"

"You sound just like your mother," she said grumpily. "Don't be so prim. An old gal with a bit of a bun isn't that much of a scandal. Half the sacred Book Class drink more than you know."

Upstairs, amid the closely packed bibelots, holding tight to my cut-crystal tumbler of whiskey, I listened to my now recovered hostess as she gazed into a small fire in her grate and told me, in sorrowful, mellifluous tones, just why she had nothing to live for.

"I know I shouldn't ask a busy young man up to my apartment to talk about myself, but for some reason you're sympathetic, and there are times when one just wants to ramble on. You will say that I'm feeling sorry for myself, and, of course, that's true, but my situation strikes me as peculiarly odious. I have no family left, unless you count my brother, Donald, who's simply praying that I won't have dissipated all my little pile before I'm gone. There are no men in my life — that's the real point. And don't tell me I could still get hold of a man, for I don't want it that way. I can't abide the picture of two old creatures clutching at each other in their loneliness. No, no, that sort of thing is for youth and beauty. I've *had* my share, and I'll never compromise!"

Leila threw back her head and stared at me as defiantly as a Christian girl telling the centurions that she prefers the lions to dishonor.

"What is there left for me? I have no profession, no aptitudes, and it's far too late for me to acquire any. I have no hobbies, except that I rather enjoy having my jewelry reset, and I like cards. Cards have helped, I admit, but I'm coming to the end of that. And as for religion — I tried being a Catholic, and I found it didn't give anything like the consolation it's supposed to. You will say it's my fault for having depended too much on men, but does it help to have things one's own fault?"

"Whoa!" I cried, my hands in the air. "Stop it! You weren't cast to be a brooding Garbo. Your role is Clara Bow!"

At least she laughed. "Chris, you're too ridiculous. But you make me feel better. Go home. I think I can sleep now. With only one of my usual pills."

The next day I met Mother for our bi-weekly lunch at the Colony Club, which was only a block from my Madison Avenue office. Justine Bannard, who was looking for a luncheon partner, asked whether she might join us, and as soon as we were seated I introduced the topic of Leila Lee.

"There's only one group of people that can arrest her descent," I advised them. "Her childhood friends. Otherwise the future is grim but clear. The fifth cocktail after the now habitual fourth, the lachrymose melancholia, the desperate midnight calls, the eventual overdose."

"Good heavens, surely we can do something to stop that!" was Justine's energetic response.

"Suppose we were social workers?" Mother asked. "What could we do about her?"

"Get her to a shrink," Justine suggested.

"So that she can talk about herself?" I retorted. "But that's all she does now. Couldn't you two listen as well as a doctor? Why don't you have lunch with her and get her to talk about herself and how it all started? You've known her forever. Maybe I could go along and act as a kind of independent referee. She's already shown that she trusts and likes me."

"But would Leila ever consent to it?" Mother inquired.

"I think she might jump at it!" Justine exclaimed, drawing up her neat stocky figure and turning her square countenance to each in turn. "What can we lose, anyway? I suggest, Cornelia, that we give it a try."

And so it came about, a week later, that we met with Leila at another lunch, not at a club or restaurant, but, for greater privacy, in our dining room at Seventieth Street. Mother and Justine were embarrassed by how to open the discussion, but I had been sure that Leila would take the situation in hand, and she did.

"So we're going to psychoanalyze me!" she exclaimed, putting both elbows on the table, her oval chin resting on the scarlet nails of her touching fingers. "It will be just the reverse of the group therapy everyone goes in for today.

Instead of three patients and one doctor, we'll have one patient and three doctors. Oh, it should be a lark! Where shall we begin?"

"Where one always does," I suggested. "At the beginning. A beginning shared by three persons at this table."

"You mean our childhood?"

"And background."

"Ah, but we didn't have the same background at all!" Leila insisted. "Not a bit of it."

"You surprise me," Mother observed. "I should have thought it was very much the same. We went to the same school. We lived only a few blocks from each other. Our mothers were friends."

"Can you imagine trying to explain to someone in Tokyo the difference between us?" Justine inquired.

"But I'm not interested in someone in Tokyo," Leila protested. "I'm interested only in what I see — or saw anyway — right here on the island of Manhattan. And it's absurd to think that the Lees were like the Gallatins or like your family, Justine. Neither you nor Cornelia can have the smallest conception of what it was like to be poor!"

"I remember how we envied your pearls!"

"My poor old pearls, Justine? That I used to borrow from Grandmother? Well, of course, the term 'poor' is relative. We were poor only compared with *you*, but that can be very important when one is brought up to keep one's eyes glued on Fifth Avenue. Oh, the Lees made a pretty good show of it — yes — we belonged to the right clubs and sent our children to the right schools, but we had no real solidity. When my father became ill and couldn't work, we almost went under. There were desperate family confabulations and last-minute loans — it was kept deadly quiet. But I always

123 ]

knew that everything could blow up any minute, and I used to think of you two, so snug and safe, with the wildest envy!"

"But your mother was the very paragon of the great lady!" Mother protested. "She had an elegance, Leila!"

"Ah, yes, poor dear, that she did. She held herself wonderfully and dressed like a fashion plate. But it was all done with spit and sealing wax."

"I guess that someone in Tokyo is going to be more and more bewildered," I put in. "Each of you, I can see, is going to insist she was lowly born while the others were the cat's meow! But I submit that we've already helped Leila a bit. Why don't we move on now to the question of men? Can you tell us, Leila, how you happened to marry George Washburn?"

"My family simply considered him the catch of catches." Leila's eyes seemed to reach nostalgically into the past. "No Lee female had ever aimed so high. And he didn't have to be caught, either. He wanted nothing so much as to pour his fate and fortune into my cupped hands!"

"Now, Leila," my mother cautioned her. "You're not going to tell us your parents *forced* you to marry George!"

"Oh, no. Nothing so crude. They wanted my happiness above anything. But Mummie could never believe that I was capable of happiness such as hers. You see, beneath her worldly front, under that miracle of grace in white, under the wide-brimmed hat and the lace parasol, behind the stage so cleverly set, and with such magic of economy, there was simply . . . well, there was a great love." Leila's voice rose to a kind of croon as she invoked the maternal ghost. "Oh, yes, make no mistake! Mother loved her Lorry Lee, amiable, not-too-lucky stockbroker that he was, kind fellow but certainly no shining wit, happy to sit on the edge of life and pleasantly smile. She could have married far better, but she asked for no more than her Lorry and the chance to make things easy and pleasant for him. She got him in everywhere, every house party, every yachting cruise, every trip on a private train! He didn't really care, nor did she, oddly enough; she cared only for his sake. It gave a beauty to their lives of which we children were always aware but from which we felt strangely excluded."

"But surely she wanted the same happiness for you, Leila."

"She didn't think me capable of it, Cornelia. She never said so, but children feel those things. She thought me a giddy thing, and she imagined that so long as I was never going to feel as deeply as she felt about a man, I might as well have one who would be able to give me all the things I wanted. She could be very worldly indeed, you see, where *other* people were concerned. And when I would tell her my doubts about George Washburn, ask her if it wasn't possible that he might be just a bit stupid, if he wasn't certainly more than a bit stuffy, she would say, oh, no more than your cousin Ted or than Bill So-and-So or than this man or that. She really did not see why, so long as I was probably destined to marry a nincompoop, it shouldn't be a rich one. And yet, one day shortly after my engagement was announced, when she found me in floods of tears, she cried out that it was probably all a mistake and that I had better get out of it. Oh, how I clung to her, how I hugged her!"

Justine broke the short silence that followed. "And *did* you break your engagement? I never knew that."

"No, of course I didn't. You'd have known if I had. You were both my bridesmaids. What happened was that on that very day George's mother arrived with two men carrying in a veritable trunkload of silver, all hopelessly engraved with the initials L.L.W. I simply collapsed! Yet even then I must give Mother credit. When Mrs. Washburn had gone, she said I mustn't throw my life away for a pile of trumpery silver. But I couldn't see it that way. I was stuck. I faced the music."

"And were you never happy with George?" Justine asked.

"It wasn't so bad at first. Had I only been able to have a baby, I might have managed it. The trouble was that George tried to make up to me for the disappointment. He said he would be a whole family to me! And when he was uxorious, poor man, he was impossible. I had been fool enough to believe, as Mother had believed of me, that I would never feel anything for another man stronger than what I felt for George, so that when that happened I was scared, petrified, actually. Here I had trapped myself into a small chamber, so to speak, with large wandering fancies, and it was a life sentence, too! And then Mother died, like poor Father, in middle age, and I was alone, without help or guidance."

"You could have called on us," Mother reminded her.

"Oh, yes, there was always the Book Class! But I'd rather have been scalded in oil than confess my errors to the Book Class. It has taken me all these decades to be able to do it today! But George was not observant — that is, I thought not. He worked hard in his family business. I had an affair. Then another. That was when we were living in Roslyn. You were there then, Justine."

"And I knew what you were up to, too."

Leila gaped. "How on earth did you know?"

"Because when we went into town for the day, you would never have lunch with me. And you wouldn't say why."

"Ah, I was very naïve! Anyway, it went on that way for years. Until finally I wanted to marry Alex Cameron. I got up the courage to ask George for a divorce, but he refused me flat. And then, when I went out to Reno on my own, he sued me for divorce in New York. On you-know-what grounds!"

"I remember very well," Justine said grimly. "He found your diary."

"And after that even Alex wouldn't have me!" Leila actually looked frightened as she recalled life's awesome conspiracy against her. "Was ever a woman so treated?"

"Why did you ever keep that silly diary?"

"And why did you leave it around?" Mother added. "I've always wanted to ask you that."

"Because I thought I was married to a gentleman!" Leila wailed. "Can you imagine a man doing a sneaky thing like that? Going through my bureau drawers and finding my own private, secret diary?"

"But you had wronged him, Leila!"

"You were the one who sued him for divorce, after all!"

"But in *Reno*, girls, in Reno! Where you can divorce a husband for trumping your ace at bridge. There's no insult to a Reno divorce. But to ruffle through a gal's stockings and sniff out her poor diary and then haul her over the coals in an odious New York court and expose all the most *intimate* things about her and let the evening papers get hold of them . . . well, who but an unmitigated cad would do that?"

"Any husband," Justine retorted.

"I'm afraid I can't blame George for that," Mother agreed. "After all, Leila, you took your chances when you were unfaithful. You have no cause to complain of what George did."

The three of them might have been girls at school again. Mother and Justine seemed completely to have forgotten the reason for our session; both were intent on making their friend see the error of her ways. Poor Leila was undone by their sudden hardness; she had assumed, for a few brief moments, that she had found an undreamed-of haven of understanding, where the Book Class was going to be as cozy as her hairdresser and nail-polisher, and now reality had come back like a big white sheet of sky overhead and everyone was shouting at her! By the time lunch was over, she was in tears, vowing that she would never come back to Mother's house, even to a regular meeting of the Class.

———

Leila, to the astonishment of her friends, adhered to the latter resolve. My little project for her betterment, it seemed, had simply speeded her on her downward path. She ceased even to appear at Blodgett's, and her brother, whom I occasionally saw at the Patroons, told me that she was now drinking dangerously. When I called on her, she treated me to a long monologue on her wrongs.

"I've always been rejected by my world, Chris; that's the long and short of it. They've always sniffed me out, found me wanting, shaken me up to make the false things they sense in me tumble out on the floor. But when they've exposed me, humiliated me, shrieked at me, will they let me go? Will they ever let me be? Never! They cling to me, drag me along with them, like some rattling old tin can tied to the rear of a newlywed's car, so that all the *other* worlds, into which I'm not allowed to escape, can see my abjection!"

"What about your second marriage, Leila?"

"Oh, don't speak of it!"

"Why shouldn't I?" I was determined to bolster my obviously failing therapy by making her face at least one fact. "From what I've been able to make out, you rather effectively managed to escape your old world there."

"Not really. I had the illusion of flight. It was not so much an escape as a nightmare. Tony Meiksel was a bootlegger whom I met in a speakeasy. Oh, the whole thing was pure Scott Fitzgerald! And just as unreal, too. I thought that he represented all the things that my soft, simpering, hypocritical old world lacked; I thought he had guts and strong feelings and a kind of cleanness in crime. But it turned out that I was only his prey. He was motivated by nothing but greed. And when I found out what he was and fled to my brother's for safety, he refused a divorce except at the price of the last penny I had in the world!"

"How did you get your divorce then?"

"Through my family! That was just the hell of it. My brother Donald and my cousin Harry Lee put a detective on him and then went themselves to trap him in a hotel where he was in bed with a blonde. I got my divorce on grounds of adultery."

"Just what you criticized Mr. Washburn for doing to you!"

"But I wasn't a crook and an extortionist!"

"You wanted a settlement, didn't you?" I can say in defense of my brutality only that I was now trying shock treatment.

"Oh, Chris, don't be such an ass. There's a difference between a lady in distress and a bootlegger!"

"All right. Go on."

129 ]

"There's nothing more to tell. That's it! Once again the family intervened to get me out — or rather to get me back. Their force was too great. I didn't try to escape again."

Poor Leila! She did try to escape again, only six months after this, and she succeeded at last, by means of an overdose of sleeping pills. Whatever the force required to keep a woman going in the world of the Book Class, she fatally lacked it, and worse still, she lacked the force to impel herself into any other.

In those last months, when she was drinking heavily enough to have provided a finale had drugs not offered a speedier one, I begged Mother and Justine to go to see her. Both declined. They were ready to pay for doctors or nurses, or any trip to a sanatorium, but they declined absolutely to see her when she was drunk and maudlin. I had seen Mother, at the Harvard-Yale boat races at New London, cheerfully supporting Manny, too inebriated to walk alone, to her car, and Justine would have done the same, I am sure, for Chuck, but a member of the Book Class was different. If Leila chose to render herself unpresentable, then she should not be presented. They would wait until she had slept it off.

Almost nobody but myself went to see Leila in those last months. She was never quite bad enough to be committed; she would simply sit for hours on end, staring at the wall and telling anyone who came in, her maid, the cleaning woman, her brother, me, that she wanted to die. And yet the prospect terrified her. Like the old black in *Showboat*, she was "tired of livin' and feared of dyin'."

I wondered why I visited her. Was it compassion or curiosity? I wanted everything to be over for her, not only for her sake but my own. The spectacle of her rejection of life had finally angered me, like the spectacle of a spoiled child smashing its toys. This precious thing had been placed in her care, and look what she was doing with it! On the day when I called and was told at the desk that she had died that morning, my first thought was that I should have to tell Mother. I foresaw with dismay that the coldness of her reaction would be the mirror of my own.

# 10

ADELINE BLOODGOOD may have been the member of the Book Class with whom I was most intimate, but Mylo Jessup was the one I loved. Yet she was never as close to me as Justine Bannard or even Georgia Bristed. Nobody, I think, was ever very close to Mylo. She adored her amiable, easygoing, utterly charming husband, Halsted, the famed polo player, and their son and daughter, who so much resembled him, but although the three of them — or at least the two men — returned her love, it was much less intensely — none of them were capable of intensity. And they could never comprehend her. Mylo lived her life amid densities of incomprehension that she never seemed to mind, possibly because she expected nothing else. Somehow she deemed it her function to feel rather than to be felt. It never occurred to her to blame people for not sharing her depths; she might even have regarded their state as a blessed exemption.

In 1958, the year of our first professional association — I became the decorator for her Bracton Village project — Mylo was sixty-six but still beautiful. She had the broad

shoulders, strong back and thin hips of the natural athlete —
which, incidentally, she was, having won national prizes as
a figure skater. Her face, heart-shaped and very pale, was
dominated by large, blue-green eyes, serene despite their
habitual expression of doubt, and her gray hair, untinted, was
bobbed in the style of the twenties, which she had never
dropped. I see her, in a portrait of the period, in profile, one
hand on her hip, her long neck held back, a type of Madonna-
like flapper, a strange combination of repose and its an-
tithesis. The Jazz Age had been hectic; Mylo was silent and
still. I have said that she was beautiful, and her figure noble,
but was she sexy? No, but not, one felt, because she couldn't
have been. She was like a Diana, chaste — yet here I am
driveling on about a woman who was six times a grandmother! The big thing about her was that she was obviously
sincere and totally honest. No matter where one might have
tapped her with a spiritual hammer, it would have rung true.

Coming home early from my office one afternoon to get
caught up on some back mail, I called at Mother's. It happened to be one of her Book Class days, but it was three
o'clock, and I assumed that the ladies would have left, as
they had, all but Mylo.

"You said you might be in early," Mother announced, as
I entered her living room. "So I suggested to Mylo that she
wait. She seems to have a job for you. Of course, I shall
expect a commission!"

"And of course you shall have it. Even though it may be
my pleasure to work for any member of the distinguished
Class for nothing. What can I do for you, Mylo?"

"I wondered, Chris, whether, busy as you are, you could
possibly manage to come up to Bracton on Saturday? I'd

promise you a very good lunch and a very dry Martini. It has to do with renovating an old house on our place. But, of course, there can be no idea of your not charging. It should be a biggish job."

"What train shall I take?"

"My car will pick you up here at eleven."

"You should have heard Mylo at lunch, Chris," said Mother now, who knew her friend well enough to be sure there would be no further talk of business until our scheduled meeting. Mylo Jessup would never intrude on a minute of anyone's "free" time. "She was absolutely brilliant about Proust. She made us feel that it was all great art, even the parts about the Baron de Charlus, which, I must confess, are a bit strong for my taste."

"Well, good for Mylo!" I exclaimed. "I thought you girls might have felt like Edith Wharton, who deplored the passage where the narrator climbs to a transom window to spy on Charlus and the tailor in what she deemed an 'unedifying scene.'"

Mylo smiled, but her smile was faintly embarrassed. "How like you, Chris! To put your finger on the one episode in all the seven novels that gives me the most trouble!"

"That was easy. The great Edith leads one directly to it. *Cherchez la puritaine!* But I feel sure, Mylo, that you are able to penetrate the heavy curtains of contemporary prejudice to enter the sanctum sanctorum of art!"

My way of approaching this remarkable woman was quite deliberate. I knew that she dwelt in the very capital of Philistia, that her husband and children were soulfully, mindlessly dedicated to the cult of sport. But I had suspected from my youth that Mrs. Jessup had never regarded me, as they undoubtedly did, as a pariah excluded from the portals of an athlete's heaven, but rather as the denizen of a voluptuous hades into which it could never be *her* good fortune to wander. That, anyway, is what I had read into the timid curiosity that seemed to glow faintly in her eyes whenever she talked to me of art or literature. She bowed to her fate; she raised her pick willingly enough to smash the rocks assigned to her chain gang; she even deplored the smoldering ashes of resentment in her own heart. Oh, yes, she made love to her life sentence, but nonetheless there must have been moments when my cracked song may have sounded like the silvery strains of Venus to Tannhäuser! Even Mother seemed to recognize this aspect of her friend's personality when she spoke of Mylo's being "naughty."

"Mylo doesn't quite like your saying that," Mother observed now. "She told us that Proust couldn't help being what he was, but that he would have been a greater novelist, perhaps even a Tolstoy, had he been a normal man."

"Did you really tell them that, Mylo?"

"Something like it. I think I suggested that Tolstoy may have seen a larger world."

"You compared that sentimental Slav to a genius like Proust? Like Peter, you denied your lord?"

"Don't mind him, Mylo, he's being perfectly ridiculous!"

"Do you believe in art at *any* price, Chris?"

"The price goes up and up," I retorted. "Read your auction news!"

"And nothing matters but beauty?" Mylo asked earnestly.

"Don't tell us Charlus is beautiful!" Mother protested.

"Nothing matters but beauty," I insisted. "And yes, Ma, Charlus *is* beautiful."

"Then you're definitely the man for my Bracton project," Mylo concluded briskly, rising to take her leave. "For that *must* be beautiful."

"Oh, stay two minutes!" I urged her. "Tell me about it. Don't worry about my not being in the office. I'll start the meter running."

"Very well. On that condition." Mylo reseated herself. "You know we moved up to Bracton after Halsted had his stroke. We wanted to get away from Long Island and the very sight of a polo field, with all its sad reminders. We found a lovely farm up there, and it's blissfully peaceful. Halsted, thank God, has full use of his hands, and he's fixed up a work room, where he does carpentry. Our land takes in part of the tiny village of Bracton, including a perfect jewel of a Greek Revival temple that is literally falling apart. The tenant died last winter, and we've decided to do it over. Halsted goes in every morning and works with two carpenters. He's having the time of his life!"

"And you want me to decorate it?"

"I want you to do more than that, Chris. I want you to help me restore it to what it was in the eighteen twenties. I want to furnish it completely in the period. With everything exactly right."

"You know that may get you into real money. Once you start on these things . . ."

"Oh, I know it!" Mylo exclaimed, with a sudden gust of feeling. "But if it amuses Halsted, what does it matter? The children have their trusts, and I don't need a penny more than I have. Why shouldn't Halsted's money be used to give him pleasure? He doesn't have so many things left that amuse him!"

Mother and I exchanged glances, both recognizing at once

that only the deepest concern could cause a woman as reticent as Mylo to mention family finances.

"No reason at all!" I responded vigorously. "Only, I didn't know that Mr. Jessup had such antiquarian tastes."

"That's what the children say," Mylo retorted, almost indignantly. "People think that just because a man has been a great athlete, he doesn't care about beautiful things. But Halsted has always had the finest natural taste. He can spot anything the least bit fussy or vulgar a mile away!"

"Well, I'm your man. We'll go right to work. By the time we've finished, that little Greek temple will be like Cleopatra's barge — burnished gold. It will burn on the water!"

After Mylo had departed, I lingered for a word with Mother.

"*Does* Mr. Jessup have natural taste?"

"If he has any, it must be that. I doubt he's ever read a book or looked at a picture in his life. But he's still the dearest of men. He'll understand that Mylo's trying to make him happy, so he'll *be* happy."

"If it kills him, you mean?"

"No, because he's a happy type, anyway. Even old and sick. It's wonderful."

"So there's nothing to be lost — but money."

"Perhaps not even that. Mylo will buy well. Isn't it your theory that she's starved her aesthetic side? To conform to the god of the Jessups? Or to what she thought was the god of the Jessups?"

"The god of polo?"

Mother seemed to debate this. "The god of sport, anyway. Or the god of the out-of-doors. The god of country life: horses and dogs. I think you may be right. Mylo comes into town to go to the Book Class like a minister sneaking off to a

137 ]

disorderly house. She has a horror of having any pleasures that Halsted and the children can't share."

"That's when, as you say, she's been 'naughty.' "

"And the sad thing is that Halsted would be just as proud of her if she were as *précieuse* as Adeline Bloodgood!"

If the farmhouse at Bracton, to which I was driven on Saturday, represented that natural good taste of Halsted Jessup, it was a fine example of it. It was long and low, gray-tiled and ivy-covered, commanding a wide view of the verdant and comfortable countryside. My genial host met me at the door with a hail and a sharp, instantly obeyed order to two barking Labradors at his sides. He was tall, straight and handsome, despite his seventy years and the steel walker that he propelled before him. He had a high forehead and a large aquiline nose; his voice was richly resonant and authoritative. Yet his eyes, mild and sky-blue, were smiling.

"Mylo will be right down. She's making up a list of things for you to help her get. Oh, you will find that she's a demon of energy! The good burghers of Bracton won't recognize the old place when she's through with it. She'll be like that czarina — who was it? — that had pretty villages erected at the stages of her proposed progresses!"

"Maybe that's what Bracton has been waiting for — a Catherine the Great. Well, I must mind my p's and q's if I don't want to be sent to Siberia."

"Oh, we'll take care of you, my boy. Stick along with Mylo and me, and you'll go places. Why, in a few years' time there won't be a soul at Colonial Williamsburg. They'll all have taken buses to Bracton! Won't they, my dear?"

For Mylo had just appeared in the hallway behind him, tense — as I could immediately feel — hesitant, but also with a hint in her eyes that she was embarking on a venture that just *might* be fun. Would that make it "naughty"? I was immediately determined to do my best to see that it wouldn't.

---

Halsted Jessup's prediction about his wife's energy was richly fulfilled in the weeks that followed. It even began to seem conceivable to me that we *were* on the path to a minor Williamsburg. In one of the warehouses to which Mylo and I now devoted many of our afternoons, I found her in deep contemplation before a white wooden commode of a singular delicacy and chasteness.

"For the upstairs corridor?" I suggested.

"I was thinking of the little church. Wouldn't it make a perfect altar?"

"Oh, are we going to do the church, too?"

"Well, why not? It needs it so!"

"One thing at a time," I cautioned her. "We must finish the temple first."

We might have been two children who had played hookey from school and were making the most of a scant bit of purloined time. I began to wonder whether feeling "naughty" wasn't Mylo's subconscious device to intensify the pleasure of this unprecedented escapade into the world of beautiful things. Her energy was limitless; she never seemed tired, even after rooms of chairs and acres of carpets. Her only compunction appeared to be for me.

"I'm taking up too much of your time, Chris," she protested, when we had seen our fortieth grandfather clock. "Your commissions aren't going to begin to pay you. You'll have to accept an expert consultant's fee."

"I'm getting rich off you, Mylo! Ask your husband."

"Well, he hasn't objected to anything yet. He says the

same thing whenever I show him a bill: 'If a thing's worth doing, it's worth doing well.' "

"An Ideal Husband!"

But this was not the right note for Mylo. Her brow was immediately puckered. "I'm doing it all for him, of course."

"Oh, of course."

Her eye was almost as sharp as mine; we rarely differed aesthetically — only in the value we gave to authenticity. She refused, for example, to buy a horsehair sofa with feet of gilded eagle claws.

"But it's precisely what you would have seen in your parlor in eighteen twenty," I pointed out. "And just look at its condition! It might have been made yesterday."

"That's because it's probably spent the last century in storage. Where it belongs. I don't want an average house of eighteen twenty. I want the best taste of the day!"

"You mean the best taste of *our* day. Second-guessing the taste of eighteen twenty. Your house will be a fantasy, Mylo."

"Ah, but it will be a beautiful one!"

Well, I could not be too disputatious about this. If she wanted to touch up the past, that was harmless enough and a small defect in an otherwise perfect client. But I had a premonition of disaster on the weekend that her daughter, Alida Huntington, came up to Bracton to inspect the progress of the work. Alida lived in Maryland, where her horse farm occupied all of her time and attention. Only a threat to her own source of funds could have explained the exhaustive and commentless tour that she made of the village structures in which her mother was planning alterations. Her first reaction was aimed directly at her father, when the four of us sat down to lunch afterwards.

"This must be costing you a pretty penny, Pa."

"No more than I have in the bank, love."

"I bet I could save our fox hunt, which is in imminent danger of dissolution, with what you're spending on a single room here!"

"No doubt. But art has its uses, too."

"Since when did you become a long-hair, old dear?"

"Since I couldn't get on a horse, reindeer."

"Shouldn't you learn to distrust sudden emotional substitutes?"

"Wait till your first stroke, baby."

"I hope it will finish me off, anyway."

"Alida!" her mother reproached her sharply.

"Oh, leave it, Ma. Pa and I understand each other. We've always been the realists of the family."

"You think I'm too old for a new interest in life?" Halsted demanded of his daughter, with something like a low growl in his gentle tone.

"I think you might find a cheaper one."

Alida was a big, raw-boned blonde whom one thought of as always in jodhpurs, brandishing a riding crop. She cared a great deal for a great many animals and a lesser amount for a small number of people. But where her father and brother were tolerant, she was bigoted. She was impatient of any values not her own and tended to sniff them out and try to extirpate them in her family and set. It is well known that women with causes are more prone to fanaticism than men. I recall when I was with the Red Cross on the beaches of Normandy, watching German war prisoners being marched aboard beached LSTs for transport to England. The soldiers would walk briskly, sometimes whistling or singing, frankly delighted that their terrible ordeal was over. But there was always a little group of German nurses, shrieking obscenities and crying "Heil Hitler" that had to be forced on to the vessels. Alida must have felt about country life as these had felt about *Lebensraum*.

"Who would ever have thought you'd end up in the museum business, Pa?" she drawled. "It shows one can never count on the future."

"It gives me something to do, Alida."

"Gives *you* something to do! I thought Mother and Christopher were the busy beavers around here."

"We work together."

"Don't you find three rather a crowd?"

"That's not the way it is at all, Alida!" her father exclaimed angrily. "Your mother and I have a joint project, and Chris is simply helping us carry it out."

"Well, it's sweet of you to put it that way, old dear, but the day you can tell an Empire *chaise longue* from a kitchen cupboard will be the day I stand up to cheer! But of course I see how it is. Ma's having a lark with your bankroll, and you're having a lark playing Santa Claus. Don't *look* at me that way. Everyone knows she's always twisted you around her little finger!"

I looked at poor Mylo. She was sitting very still, her large reproachful eyes fixed on her daughter. Halsted, his cheeks now a mottled red, was almost shouting.

"I tell you, Alida, your mother and I are in this thing together! You've always regarded me as an ass, but there's no law that says a man *has* to stay one!"

"But Alida is absolutely *right*," Mylo intervened in a low voice, staring down now at the table. "I've done it all for my own selfish reasons. I've been fooling myself that it was a kind of therapy for you, darling." To my utter dismay I saw the big tears in Mylo's eyes. "And all the while you've seen it, too, and have tried to convince me the therapy was working. Oh, yes, it's true what Alida says! You'd do *anything* to give me pleasure. Even if my only real pleasure is giving you some. But, darling, we don't need to spend your money for that. We can save it for our grandchildren. Alida is quite right! I'm a frustrated aesthete who's dressing up her fantasies as a marital duty. Well, it's over, that I promise you! Christopher, please cancel everything that can still be cancelled. The project is finished."

"Mylo!" cried her husband.

But Mylo had left the table, and I knew that the door she slammed behind her was as final as Nora's in *A Doll's House.* The project, as she had said, was finished.

"I hope you're satisfied with this day's work, Alida," her father said. Yet he said it with a surprising mildness. He was evidently a man who had learned to accept the quixotic violence of the other sex.

Mylo did not reappear, and Alida and I took the same train to New York. Even she seemed a bit taken aback by the extremity of her mother's reaction. But after a bit she resumed her normal bad manners.

"It's too bad for you, of course, Chris. You'll have lost a tidy bit of business. Still, you must have made something pretty good out of it by this time."

"You think that's why I encouraged your mother? For the commissions?"

"Why on earth not? It's your business, isn't it?"

"Certainly it's my business. But in this case it was also my joy."

"Well, that was nice, wasn't it? An extra dividend."

"It was. I was happy to see your mother realizing a side of her personality that she has suppressed too long."

"You think her a natural spendthrift?"

"I think her a natural artist."

"And to be a natural artist one must romp through the family exchequer?"

"You'll get back every penny she spent, Alida. And double."

"You seem to forget that Daddy has been talking about setting the place up as a museum. How would I ever get *that* back?"

"In dividends of satisfaction at being part of a great public cause."

"I'm sorry to be such a philistine. I prefer hard cash."

"Oh, you're something more than a philistine, Alida."

"And what is that?"

"A bitch. Being such an animal lover, you can take that as a compliment."

And with this I got up to take a seat across the aisle from her.

———

Mylo, of course, was good to her word. Never again did she buy a pretty thing. When Halsted died, only two years after our abortive experiment at Bracton, she surprised everyone by releasing her interest in his estate to the children and moving into a small apartment in town. It was an attractive apartment — everything she had anything to do with she made attractive — but it was very simple, compared with her former lodgings, and she decorated it entirely with her old things. I doubt that she even bought a new lampshade. She certainly did not buy one through me.

I sometimes dropped in to have a cocktail with her on my way to a dinner party. She aged very well, maintaining her slim, muscular figure and the fine lines of her face. She was always her old disciplined self, smiling, cheerful, faintly impersonal. Only once in the next decade did we talk intimately, and then it was she who broached the topic.

"You must have sometimes wondered, Chris, why I reacted so violently to Alida's criticism of our project at Bracton."

"I always knew there was a hand that was holding you back. Are you going to tell me whose it was? Not Alida's, certainly."

"I am going to let you read about it."

"You mean you've written a book? Ah, the glorious Class! I always knew that, between you, you'd produce one."

"Not a book, certainly not. A short memoir. I've had a lot of time to think things out, and I've written some of them down. As they came to me, alive, even with conversations, although these must be very much imagined. Still, the gist, I believe, is there. I don't know *why* I was the way I was, and I'm too old to be psychoanalyzed. But I think I see *how* I was. And there it is." She indicated a little stack of manuscript on the table before us. "You may take it and read it. It won't keep you but an hour. Some day you can bring it back to me. You may be my only reader."

"May I ask why I am so privileged?"

"Because you tried to help me once. As only one other person has ever done."

I hesitated. "Your husband?"

"Oh, no. He didn't help me. He was my life."

I picked up the papers as I arose to depart. "I'll read it tonight."

And here it is.

# 11

THE MOST IMPORTANT PERSON in my youth — no, let me put it even more strongly — the most important person in such life as I had before I dedicated it to Halsted Jessup was Rick Wise. What am I saying? More important than my father and mother, than my two younger brothers, than my grandmother, my old nurse, Aggy, and all my aunts and uncles? Yes! And how could that be true of a good little brownstone girl? But if it was not unusual, I should not be taking pen in hand to write this memoir.

I was first tempted to put it that Rick, in my nineteenth and twentieth years, *was* my life, but that is not really so. It would be more accurate to say that he was everything that was *not* my life, that he was something more like an answer or antidote to life, something that could be counted on to keep me going when everything else seemed flat and pointless — and when the flatness and pointlessness was nobody's fault but my own. To Father and my uncles, on the other hand, and, even to a large extent, to Mother, Rick was simply a Jewish boy.

He was, however, a very special kind of Jew. His mother

was a Gentile, a Protestant; indeed, she was my mother's second cousin, a Van Sinderen, who, according to my family, had chosen a disgraceful alternative to an impoverished old-maidhood by marrying the great investment banker Jacob Wise. And Mr. Wise, indeed, appeared to agree with them, for he always treated his plain, fluttery, dull little spouse as if he despised her for mating with the "likes of him." There were two stout, sensible, dark-featured, dull daughters, who equally failed to interest him, and last, but far from least, the pale, ailing, raven-haired, beautiful Rick, whom he uncritically adored.

My father, left to himself, would have had nothing to do with the Wises. He was a consistent anti-Semite, though his anti-Semitism was diluted and almost lost in the broad, smug sea of his near universal disesteem for his fellow men. There was little animosity in this casual contempt; he simply believed, with a shrug of his shoulders, that outside a handful of New York, Boston and Philadelphia Episcopalian families who dated back to the Revolution, the human race was a harmless but ridiculous institution. He protected himself from undesirable shoulder-rubbings by spending that part of his days not required by the sale of municipal bonds at the Knickerbocker Club, where his handsome, ruddy figure was to be seen sitting stiffly at the bridge table or standing stiffly at the bar. When Mother entertained at dinner she would always telephone the doorman of the club at seven o'clock to remind Father to come home in time to dress.

She, on the other hand, represented a good deal of what was best in old New York. She was shrewd, down-to-earth, efficient, with a zest for life almost inconsistent with the neatness of her attire and the correctness of her demeanor. Everything about Mother, from her strong, regular features to her deep abdominal chuckle, suggested a park that achieved gracefulness by being well cut and well fenced. She was utterly conventional, but convention to her was a kind of game. She might have thought that her cousin Abby had not done well to marry Jacob Wise, but Abby was her kin, and family loyalty was a cardinal rule of the game. Father could huff and puff as he would, but rules were rules, and she blandly ignored him.

I might say a word here of the matriarchal aspect of old New York. Mother and her sisters lived on the "remnants," as they ungratefully put it, of what had once been a handsome fortune, derived from the China trade. They had married men who preferred clubs and horses to Wall Street. If the latter all worked in banks or brokerage houses, they didn't work very hard, nor, I imagine, very profitably. There must have been a tacit understanding between the sisters that if their ship was to stay afloat, it would have to be through their management. Men were capable, no doubt, of making fortunes, but they were not great hands at preserving them, and if one had not married a "tycoon," like one's grandfather, but an easygoing "clubbable" type, it behooved one to take the lead in keeping accounts and regulating expenses.

Children rapidly perceive where the real power lies, and I was never deceived by the lip service that Mother rendered to her blustering spouse. It was thus that I knew that my special friendship with Rick Wise was safe — at least from Father. The only thing that threatened it was the poor boy's own health. He suffered from a weak heart, and it was not supposed, as my old nurse used brutally to put it, that he would make "old bones."

It was easy for me to visit him, for he lived on the same

street. The Wise mansion, as it was always appropriately called, was on the corner of Fifth Avenue; it was a great gray French Renaissance château, handsome enough on the outside but dark and gloomy within, despite the illuminated canvases of Mr. Wise's collection of Spanish and Italian masters. My family occupied a brownstone in the middle of the block that Elsie de Wolfe had modernized as much as she could, given the limitation of Mother's stubborn refusal to part with her Victorian relics. The great decorator used to insist that our modest home was one of her masterpieces, explaining, if anyone expressed surprise, "You don't know what I had to *keep!*"

Indeed, our interior was like Mother's soul: sentiment at war with taste. She was always being bothered by her own soft-heartedness. She worried about Rick as she might have worried about abandoned bibelots. When the doctors condemned him, after the age of twenty, to spend two out of three days in bed or on a couch, she arranged with Cousin Abby Wise that I should spend one afternoon a week reading aloud to him or playing games. When Father stipulated that Rick's door should always be left open during my visits, Mother simply asked coldly why anyone should want to close it.

Rick, two years older than I, was a youth of extraordinary sensitivity and penetration. He would fix his large burning dark eyes upon me and listen gravely until my innermost thoughts seemed to have been magnetized right out of me. His body, wrapped in red or blue silk, would be absolutely still, the long, emaciated arms folded on his chest. He might have been an alabaster box in the shape of a man, some curious delicate work of ancient art harboring a flame within that revealed itself only in the flicker in his eyes. Yet the flame must have been consuming him. I came to regard him with something like awe.

"That's just because you've been told that I'm dying," he retorted when I confessed this.

"Oh, don't say that!"

"Why not? We're all dying — every day we live. I shall probably survive a considerable number of people who are feeling very sorry for me. I don't say it's easy to die — it isn't — but it's certainly easier if one's natural about it."

"And you feel that people aren't? I mean friends and family? *Me?*"

"Well, everybody is very kind. They lower their voices when they come in here and try to think of pleasant things to say. But I can feel their revulsion. To them this room is an antechamber of death. If this couch were moved to an African veldt, I should soon spot the black wings of a vulture hovering overhead. And in a way that might be better. Because the vulture would be attracted, not repelled, by my state. I could feel that my demise would be a gain for at least one living creature."

"Oh, Rick, please, that's too horrible!" I cried, miserably upset. "I can't bear it!" But then, as he simply stared coolly at me, I made myself recognize that I was being no help to him. The least I could do was to try to face his fate as squarely as he did.

"All right. I tell you what. I'll be a kind of vulture! Oh, you're going to get well, I know, but as long as you think it's fatuous to talk that way, I won't. Let me start by learning things from you. All kinds of wonderful things that you know and I don't. Then if anything *should* go wrong, I could say that there *had* been one living creature, Mylo Bowen, who had profited from your ordeal."

[ 150

"Why, Mylo, that's darling of you! But what could I teach you? Aren't you right up at the top of your class at Miss Chapin's?"

"Oh, Rick, don't laugh at me! You know you're cultivated to your fingertips. You know everything about art and literature. Look at this house. It's a museum! And your room . . . why, I don't know what half the things in here are. What's that picture over the desk, for example, the orchid with the hummingbirds?"

"It's a Martin Heade."

"You see? I've never even heard of him."

"Neither had Daddy. But then Daddy doesn't recognize American painters. As a matter of fact, he doesn't recognize any painter after Velásquez."

"All right. Let's take Velásquez. What do I know about Velásquez? Did he paint that gaunt monk in the corridor to the dining room?"

"No, but he might have. That was Zurbarán. You weren't far off. How about this, Mylo? I'm not such an ass as to think I could be your teacher, but maybe I could supply some moral backing to help you educate yourself. You ought to go to college."

"Father says that girls who go to college don't get to the altar."

"Well, who cares about altars? Don't stifle your brain because of Cousin Alfred's prejudices. Talk to your mother."

"But she feels the same way. Mother says a woman can learn all she needs from books, without having some old maid in glasses lecture to her."

Rick pounced on this. "Then you've discussed it with her. You've told her you want to go!"

"Oh, we've discussed it, yes. I've even talked about it with

Miss Chapin. She said that if I wanted to go to Barnard, I'd have to transfer to Brearley for the rest of the school year. Brearley, apparently, prepares you for the college requirements."

"Which Miss Chapin disdains to do? And they call that education! Mylo, if you don't throw down the gauntlet now, you'll be lost forever. You'll muffle your brain and marry some stockbroker and spend the rest of your days trying to be as stupid as he!"

"And we talk about *you* not having a future!"

Rick reached over suddenly to seize my hand in his cold ones. "It's not too late, Mylo. It's not too late!"

"What's not too late, my children?"

Mr. Wise, huge, stout, grinning, loomed in the doorway.

"Rick wants to prepare me for college, Cousin Jacob," I said, quick now to implement my new inspiration. "He's offered to be my tutor."

"I call that an excellent idea!"

"It's no such thing, Dad. I'm not qualified."

"Why on earth not?"

"I'm no more qualified than *you* are. Neither you nor I live in the modern world."

"Oh? And where, pray, do I live?" Rick's father always adopted the same humble, bantering tone with his often acidulous son.

"You live in the Renaissance! Though why, I can't imagine. You and I would have been put in ghettos then."

"I care about beauty, my boy," his father answered patiently.

"You care about opulence! You care about things that gleam and glitter!" It always distressed me that the more his father demeaned himself, the more Rick berated him.

"You have no taste for natural things. Look at that little beach scene. It's a Kensett. Of course, like all Kensetts, it needs a stronger light . . ."

"Can I get you one?" his father asked eagerly.

"Never mind that now. I'm trying to make a point. My pictures are not of golden interiors, palaces and cathedrals, silks and satins. They show the real world!"

"It's very true. They're mostly out-of-doors." Cousin Jacob nodded in recognition as he turned to the Winslow Homer. "I suppose that's only natural, if you have to be cooped up in here."

"My pictures bring me all I miss."

"Oh, my boy, do you suppose the doctors would let me take you out west in a private railway car?" There was almost a sob now in Cousin Jacob's tone. "I could make you perfectly comfortable, and we'd see the prairies and the Rockies. I'd bring a doctor and a nurse and anything you needed. Shall we risk it?"

Rick smiled sourly at me. "Daddy thinks it's unfair that his money can't buy me a longer life."

"Don't talk like that!" Jacob Wise shouted suddenly, waxing very red in the face. "Don't say such terrible things! I forbid you!"

Why was Rick so cruel to his father? Because the old man was bursting with the life he lacked? Or because he knew that Jacob Wise would have scorned him had he been plain and female, like his sisters? I think it was the latter. I think Rick could not value a paternal love that was made up of pride of possession.

"Oh, Daddy, go away, please, if you're going to shout. You know I can't stand noise."

The poor man seemed broken by this, and after looking

from one to the other of us in a kind of beseeching perplexity, he shuffled out of the room.

"Rick, you shouldn't be so horrible to him!"

"Don't be tiresome, Mylo. It is not only the young who must learn manners."

I could not bear his tone, and my indignation gave me the courage to pursue his father down to his library. I found him slumped over his great black Italian table-desk, his face covered by his hands. When he heard my step, he looked up wildly, as if he didn't know me.

"Cousin Jacob!" I exclaimed. "He doesn't mean to hurt you."

"What do *I* matter, my dear?" He startled me by jumping up suddenly to seize both my hands. "Don't go to college, please! Let him teach you! He knows everything. Really, he does. Come here every afternoon. It will give him an interest in living. It may even save him!"

———

Cousin Jacob's idea matched perfectly with my own. I suffered from the notion — almost at times the obsession — that I was of no real use to anybody. Father lived for his clubs and his few devoted friends; Mother for the satisfaction of her own efficient coping with the problems of her household; my younger brothers, extroverts both, had been absorbed first with their school athletics and then with girls and drinking. I had occasionally taken on tasks for one of Mother's charities, but the vision that had arrested me, romantically, perhaps absurdly, from the age of thirteen, had been of sacrificing myself, not for a group or even for a cause, but for a person, usually a man. It did not have to be a young man. In one of my fantasies I followed an old priest to a leper colony; in another I destroyed my health in a voluntary experiment for a great medical pioneer.

And now I was intensely excited by the idea that my day-dreaming may not, after all, have been only that, that here was a reality, at my very doorstep, waiting to be taken up. But I still had to be crafty. Too much was at stake. When I put my Barnard proposal to Papa, I did so in a way that would make it peculiarly repellent to him. I suggested that I found our home atmosphere stuffy and unenlightened. Later I was able to say to Mother: "Papa seems terribly angry about the Barnard plan. Really, I don't want to give him a stroke. Anyway, I'm not ready for it yet. Miss Chapin says so."

"What do you have in mind? Changing to Brearley?"

"Why go to another school when there's a great tutor a few doors away? Rick can help me. And his father thinks the occupation might be just the thing for him."

My heartbeat quickened as I took in Mother's searching glance. "Wouldn't your father mind that more than Barnard?"

"He wouldn't care if people didn't know. And why should they? Oh, Mother!" I knew I took a chance in pleading. She distrusted anything that a child wanted too much. But I was suddenly desperate. "If there's *anything* we can do for poor Rick, shouldn't we do it?"

Mother's stare seemed a curtain over conflicting thoughts. "I'll think about it."

It was agreed at length as a compromise that I should go to the Wises' three mornings a week. Rick, once persuaded, took his new duties very seriously indeed and suggested to

Mother that he instruct me in physics and chemistry, in which disciplines I was totally deficient. But, safely alone with him, I boldly announced my plan.

"I don't give a fig about going to college," I explained. "I want to learn only the things *you* care about. That's all the education I need. For you to talk to me about art and music and history. And for me to read to you from your favorite books when you're tired."

He chuckled, but I thought there was a little glitter in his dark eyes. "Ah, my poor Mylo, you want to be an aesthete! Beware!"

"Why should I?"

"Because you, my dear, *are* going to live!"

From that day on it became increasingly apparent that Rick was not. He failed rapidly during the year of our sessions and was unable to receive me on at least a third of the days scheduled. Often he was so tired that he would lie back on his couch, his eyes closed, as I read to him. Yet his attention never wandered. If I made a mistake, or accented a line of poetry wrongly, he would raise a languid hand to interrupt me.

"Take that again, dear. Start from the word . . ."

It was a wonderful time for me, for I had the occasional assurance that I brought him some release from pain. His poor old frantic father, often hovering in the corridor, afraid to interrupt us and irritate the prickly patient, would escort me to the front hall door when I left, anxiously asking whether I could detect any improvement or remission. His mother and sisters treated me as a kind of superior nurse with a special gift for comforting the ill. It was always an ugly shock to get home and be greeted by my father's invariable "Well, dear? How are things in High Jewry?"

[ 156

Small wonder that I was so happy to get back to Rick's little chamber (little only by contrast to the great ones on the *piano nobile*), with its books and flowers and pictures! God forgive me for having known perfect happiness only with the dying! But there was an ineffable quality to the peace within those four walls that kept out not only our parents but the whole rough, brash, uncomprehending city. We read Shakespeare and Henry James and Hawthorne and Montaigne; Keats and Shelley and Wordsworth. When Rick felt well enough, he would talk about everything from Assyrian inscriptions to the French Impressionists. How had he read so much, seen so much, in only twenty-one years?

At last there came a whole month in which I could not see him, and when next I went to his house it was to his bedroom and not his study that I was admitted. He was so marble-white and emaciated that he seemed almost a corpse. But his voice was still clear.

"I want you to read me *Macbeth*, Mylo. It is about persons preoccupied with death who have never learned to live. It should make me feel superior."

I had never much liked this bloody play, and I particularly disliked Lady Macbeth. Rick must have detected this in the way I read her lines:

... Come to my woman's breasts,
And take my milk for gall, you murdering ministers ...

I paused, seeing him smile, to ask him why.

"Because everything about you is so unlike Lady Macbeth, and yet there's something in the way you read that verse that makes me wonder."

"You think I may have murder in me?"

157 ]

"No. But neither did she. She couldn't do it, at the last moment."

"But she smeared the faces of the grooms with blood! She was an accessory."

"That she was. And perhaps that's what you might be, Mylo. An accessory. Lady Macbeth didn't want the crown for herself. She wanted it for *him*. And when she saw it had brought him only misery, she went to pieces. Keep her fate in mind, my dear. That will always be your danger. To live for others. They're never worth it."

"What should I live for, Rick?"

"Beauty."

"And where do I find it?"

"Anywhere you look. If you know how to look."

I glanced about at his things. "I think you've found it here."

"A little."

"And your father has it all over the house."

"But he doesn't see it! Father's purchases are what Veblen calls 'conspicuous consumption.' He thinks the tragedy of my illness is that I shall not have accomplished anything. That my early promise will be unfulfilled. And yet in some ways I have already accomplished as much as I ever should have. I doubt, for example, if I lived to sixty, that I should feel *Hamlet* or *Lear* more intensely than I do today."

"You should write down what you feel about Shakespeare, Rick. Or even dictate it to me."

"Why?"

"Because it would be an inspiration to others."

"There you go, you see? It's always 'others.' I guess you'll never be a true aesthete, after all. But you will certainly be

[ 158

an aesthete *manquée*." For a long time those large black eyes took me in. "I don't envy you, my dear," he said gravely. "Even in my state I don't envy you."

For some reason his words brought me a strange exhilaration. Then he went on, "You don't really believe in the subjective appreciation of a work of art, do you?"

"You mean I don't believe it exists?"

"You don't believe it has any value."

"Well, it seems rather selfish, doesn't it? I mean, if it's purely subjective? Shouldn't one share it? Isn't that where its value comes in?"

"Not necessarily. If Shakespeare and I meet in a single moment of actual communication, that is art. That is *Hamlet*."

"I wonder whether I will ever feel that."

"I hope not. For if you do, it may be too late."

The next morning early I awakened to find Mother standing silently by my bed.

"It's all over for Rick," she said gravely when she saw that my eyes were open. "I hope it may console you a little to know that his father sent me a line to say that you, more than anyone else, had helped Rick in the past year and a half."

It is not the purpose of this memoir to expatiate on my private grief. Suffice it to say that my parents treated me with what, for them, was great gentleness, and that my father, for at least two weeks, desisted at table from anti-Semitic remarks. But one morning at breakfast my exemption was abruptly ended. Mother looked mildly stern as she filled my coffee cup.

"Your Aunt Alice tells me that you declined her dinner

for the fourteenth. I didn't know you had an engagement that night."

"An engagement? How could I?"

"And why, pray, should I take the blankness of your social calendar for granted?"

"Because I'm not going out. I can't."

"You can't?"

"I consider myself in mourning."

"In mourning?" Mother's dramatically raised eyebrows had certainly been planned. "For whom, may I ask? It can't be for poor Rick. One doesn't mourn third cousins, except perhaps in Peking."

"My mourning is not formal," I protested indignantly. "It's in the heart!"

"Then I suggest you keep it there. It has certainly no place in society. I am not questioning your grief, my child, nor the propriety of your feeling it. But we have to base our standards on the customary rather than the unusual. It's perfectly possible, of course, to care more for a remote relation, or even a friend, than for a person within the permitted mourning category. But that must be one's private affair. Otherwise we should live in a world of incomprehensible crape."

"But I don't *want* people to know I'm in mourning! I don't care whether they think I have a sorrow or not! I just don't want to go to parties while my heart is full of Rick."

"Is that what you told your Aunt Alice?"

"I told her I didn't feel like going out."

"Do you want to get a reputation for being moody and eccentric? It's a very easy one to acquire, my girl, but you'll find it's a hard one to drop. I have been entirely frank with your aunt. I told her all about your friendship with Rick and just how you feel. I also told her that you have now pulled yourself together and that you would be happy to go to her dinner."

"Mother, I won't!"

Mother was now at her most severe. Her lips formed a straight, tight line before she spoke. "I want you to listen to me very carefully, Mylo. I am not going to give you orders about your social life. That would be absurd. You are perfectly at liberty to walk out of this house and set yourself up, if you can, on your grandmother's little trust fund. I do not purport to command or even to beseech. I simply ask you to play fair. I have raised no objection in the past year and a half to your constant association with Rick Wise. I have, with considerable difficulty, prevailed upon your father not to make scenes about it. I have represented you to the whole family as a kind of loving and devoted nurse to a dying boy. I have tried to explain what would otherwise have been deemed quixotic conduct. Very well. Now it is over. Poor Rick is gone, and there is nothing more we can do for him. Don't you think, now, that you owe *me* something? I have seen things your way. Isn't it time you saw them mine?"

Oh, it was all so fair, so brilliantly fair! Mother seemed to represent a tall, clean white force in life, looming inexorably over my past and future. There was no evading her except in the shadows, and what business had I skulking in the shadows? Society to Mother was a handful of rules, arbitrary perhaps, but useful, that kept one physically clean and morally decent. It was not until much later that it occurred to me that she had gambled on Rick's early death when she had approved our meetings. But had I flung this at her, might she not have retorted, "I still took my chance, didn't I? He could have lived twenty years!"

Of course, I went to Aunt Alice's dinner, and, of course, I found myself seated next to Halsted. I had known him, but only scantly; it had never occurred to me that he could be interested in a girl who cared for art and poetry, who smelled, so to speak, of libraries. But my life changed that night when he leaned over to me and uttered these words in that soft, melodic tone that offered so soothing a contrast to his great physical build: "I want to tell you straight off that I've heard what a wonderful friend you were to Rick Wise. And how you made his last year as painless as possible. I know this isn't party chatter, but I can't help telling you how fine I think that is."

My eyes filled at once with tears. "You knew Rick?"

"Oh, only a little bit, when we were very young. His family had the camp next to ours in the Adirondacks. He was never strong, of course, poor fellow, but I used to take him out fishing with me. I remember how bright he was. Why do you suppose God matched a brain like his with a sick body and gave such blooming health to a goon like me?"

Do I have to write any more to explain why I fell in love with Halsted? Why, almost overnight, my sense of mission was shifted from Rick, who had no more need of it, to this large, generous man? A poet's aide, an athlete's aide, what was the essential difference at the level of aiding? But looking back today I can see that I may not have been quite so subservient as I imagined, that there may be elements of aggression behind a woman's need to support a man. And I think I can see something else, too: that Mother may have sensed this in me. Halsted's mother and she were the greatest pals, and there was a good deal of concern in the Jessup family that he was seeing too much of a certain designing divorcée. Is it inconceivable that these two clever women put their heads together to substitute a pitiable girl for a mercenary one? They knew that a gullible male is the natural prey of either. If they gave me a start, could they not count on me to do the rest?

# ──◦❊ 12 ❊◦──

 IN 1961, my forty-first year, I had the opportunity, at even closer quarters than usual, to observe a crisis in the Book Class, most of whose members were by then on the shady side of seventy. The crisis, I fear, was aggravated by my own bad judgment. It involved a question of sex, not, I hasten to add, in the Class itself, but between two of its offspring.

It began — at least my role in it — at lunch on a freezing February noon. I had become weary of those long, rich midday meals in expensive midtown restaurants that are the favorite indoor sport of the design and fashion worlds, and I had adopted the habit of reserving a regular table for six months at a time at one or another of the stylish eateries within easy walking distance of my shop on Sixty-third Street. To this café I would resort daily, sometimes with one of my associates, sometimes alone, but more often with a friend or friends who would simply propose themselves to my efficient secretary, Miss Angus; she knew exactly whom I would be glad to see and who would fit with whom. That winter I had a secluded table at the Villandry, in an alcove not too distastefully decorated with murals of the châteaux on the Loire.

"Mr. Bannard will lunch with you at one," Miss Angus informed me. "But there's to be no one else. He has something private to discuss with you."

Had I first met Chuck Bannard at my then age, the prospect of such a meal *à deux* might have bored me, but he was still invested with a remnant of the romance of his football image at Chelton, where I had considered myself privileged to be his friend. Because of a difficult client I was a few minutes late, and Chuck's handsome but fleshening face was already a touch pink as he finished off what I divined had not been his first cocktail.

"I may as well give it to you straight, Chris. I've fallen horribly in love, and if Jill won't give me a divorce to marry Margot Travers, I think I'm going to split in two!"

That this was a shock is to put it mildly. It may come as something of a surprise to the reader, who will have correctly surmised that my table at the Villandry had witnessed confessions of many vices in polite society, that so common or garden a variety of proposed divorce and remarriage should have caused me the slightest consternation. But these matters derive their relative innocence or guiltiness from their context, and the context here for me was that both the defaulting husband and his presumed mistress were "Book Class babies."

Margot Travers, daughter of Polly, the political member of the Class, though her more recent espousal of Moral Rearmament may have turned her into the religious one, was a pretty but very serious, dark girl (as I still thought of her), thirty years of age, a decade younger than Chuck and the real baby of the Class. Mr. Travers, constantly unfaithful to his noble-minded, cause-adopting spouse, had been just as constantly reconciled, leaving in each case a pledge of his renewed fidelity, of which Margot had been the last. She had three considerably older brothers, big, beefy stock-broker types, like their old man, whose delinquency had been expressed, in accordance with the mores of their gen-eration, more in multiple marriages than in adulteries. Small wonder that Mrs. Travers, whose idealism had made her the butt of her family's coarse jokes, though her fortune was the major source of their revenues, had sought relief in good works. Margot, however, differed from her brothers. She had become the superefficient man Friday to the executive director of a large foundation and had earned a wide respect for the thoroughness of her research and the judiciousness of her recommendations. To the surprise of the Book Class, she had never married or even been known to have a boy friend; Leila Lee, of course, had assumed that she was a lesbian. But now it appeared that she was one of those tense intellectual women who fall for dull males just past their prime.

"And we all thought you and Jill were so happy!" I exclaimed.

"There's a difference between a happy marriage and a tepid one. I know I have nothing to reproach Jill with, and of course everyone will say I'm behaving like a snake. But you remember, Chris, how little I played the field before Jill and I were engaged. All my time at Yale I never took another girl out — she came to both proms with me. And of course we got married right after graduation. Oh, sure, I *thought* I knew what I wanted. But a man can't know what he wants at twenty-two. I'd never felt anything like what I feel now! I hadn't supposed I ever would, or maybe I hoped that what I felt for Jill was 'passion.' I never dreamed this could happen to me!"

Was it so? Could Chuck feel passion? As I glanced into those mild brown eyes, it seemed to me that perhaps there *was* a flicker of yellow in them. I couldn't be sure. Then the waiter came, and I took my time ordering to give myself a chance to assemble my thoughts.

Jill Bannard was certainly a cool woman: neat, quiet, soberly dressed, with never a blond hair out of place. She always had a pleasant word to say to everybody, and if she seemed to keep herself a bit in the background, even at her own parties, it was because she was keeping an eye on the machinery that had to function at any successful social gathering. Jill was high on "maintenance," but then somebody must be. She had picked Chuck early in the game as precisely the mate she wanted, and he had given her no reason to suppose that the day would ever come when he would crave something gamier. Everyone had always exclaimed at what a perfect pair they were. One thing, anyway, was certain. Chuck was going to have a devil of a time with his sons, both in their teens. Jill was the kind of mother, dry-eyed and stoical under assault, whose boys would adore her. I mentioned this to him now.

"Of course, I know it's going to be hard," he conceded. "But the boys are past the impressionable age. One's at Yale and one's at Chelton. They ought to be able to handle this. And their age group believes in sexual freedom. It's love, love, love, all the time."

"Ah, yes, but they judge their parents by different standards."

"Well, I can't help it. If they're going to hate me, I'll

167 ]

have to take it, that's all. In time they'll understand. But come what may, Chris, I'm not going to give Margot up. She's my first chance for real happiness. How can I turn my back on that? And for what? To save Jill a heartache she's bound to get over? And the boys some temporary discomfiture? Does God require it? Is there a god? I've become convinced that if you don't look after yourself in this life, nobody else is going to. And if you give up joy, what happens? You die joyless, and you're a long time dead. Oh, I have some morals, of course. A man shouldn't murder or steal or beat people up. But Margot, damn it all, is *my* business!"

"I see there's no arguing with you. All I might point out is that Jill may *not* get over it. And that it wouldn't kill you and Margot to wait until your boys are a bit older. You could carry on your intrigue in the meantime. I'm sure Jill would be accommodating so long as her home was preserved."

"But what about Margot?" Chuck demanded indignantly. "Don't I have to think of her? What's *she* had out of life? Mightn't she like to have a baby before she's too much older?"

I looked up. "Perhaps she's having one already. Is that the point?"

"No, no, Chris. We're not so careless."

I shrugged. "Well, I see you've made up your mind. Where do I come in? Isn't it a matter now for the lawyers? Jill's, I presume, will take you to the cleaners."

He scowled at the notion. "Here's where you come in, Chris. Margot, like me, has the greatest faith in you. She says that nobody has more influence with the Book Class. She thinks you could persuade her mother to see the whole thing from a modern point of view, and then Mrs. Travers might have some influence on *my* mother. After all, they're oldest friends."

"Your mother, I take it, is opposed."

"Opposed isn't the word for it! She's thrown in her lot with Jill, lock, stock, and barrel."

"That sounds like Justine. And Margot's mother — is she against you, too?"

"Well, you know how Mrs. Travers is. Always up in the clouds with some new cause. It's almost impossible to get her to discuss anything practical."

"It looks rather dim, doesn't it? And Jill, of course, refuses pointblank to give you a divorce."

"Not pointblank, no. In fact, at first she seemed almost willing. Unhappy, but willing. After all, who really wants a husband who has to be locked in every night?"

"Plenty of women."

"Anyway, she was almost at the point of agreeing to a divorce — that is, if the property settlement could be worked out — when Ma barged in and put her back up!"

I laughed. "As they say, with friends like your mother, what do you need enemies for?"

"Will you have lunch with Margot and Mrs. Travers? Oh, Chris, say you will!"

"What can we lose? If they'd care to join me at this table tomorrow at one, I shall be happy to buy them a very good lunch. Further than that, deponent sayeth not."

"You're a brick, Chris!"

And so it came about that I played host the following day to Margot and Polly Travers. Margot, when tense, became very severe; an observer at another table might have thought that she was passing judgment on the older woman who sat between us.

"Isn't that May Chalmers over there?" Polly asked. "I really should speak to her. She's just joined the movement, and I've been hoping she'd loan us her place in Roslyn for the June rally."

"Mother, please! We're not here to discuss Moral Rearmament. Now leave Mrs. Chalmers alone and concentrate on *me*. For once in your life. Don't worry. I shan't keep you long."

Polly Travers was as handsome as an elderly woman can be who lacks — and always has lacked — any element of sex appeal. She was tall and slender and had a fine Greek profile with a long nose that seemed to start at her marble forehead and thick gray hair, virgin to the permanent wave, that was pulled back over her scalp and tied in a bun at the nape of her neck. Her clothes were out of fashion, but had obviously once been expensive; they seemed to mock her attempts at simplicity. Polly was always trying to shake off a naturally aristocratic air. You could see it in the way she stooped to conceal her tallness (a habit of childhood, no doubt developed to mitigate the critical glances of a worldly mother) and in the way she inclined her head, as if to acknowledge some obeisance that she neither desired nor believed herself to deserve. The same high air was detectable in the scrupulous way in which she concentrated her features into a look of utter attention, lest her interlocutor should suspect that a person born a Wadsworth might consider him not worth listening to. But above all it revealed itself in her beautifully articulated syllables — she sounded a bit like Adeline Bloodgood — and in her unconscious avoidance of any slang or even any current expressions. Polly was at ease only with large audiences. Then the diffidence would fall away; the tall figure would straighten out and the spirit would soar. In private, as now, her china-blue eyes had a note of apology, as if anticipating some hinted accusation of social superiority, but behind this humility there still gleamed a small stubborn lamp of resistance to the possibility of any requested compromise in her principles — the mark of the fanatic.

"The reason I've proposed this lunch with Chris," Margot continued, "is that I want him to help you to see my situation in the light of the world we happen to be living in and not the world in which you grew up."

"I think I've shown that I know something about the world we live in, dear," Polly observed mildly.

"As far as other people are concerned, yes. But I'm speaking of family. You tend to be more conservative there."

"Do you think I was so backward about your brothers' divorces?" Polly suddenly appealed to me. "You know all about *them*, Chris. Was I such a mossback?"

I chuckled. "On the contrary. I should say you'd been tolerant to a fault."

"But that's because nothing was asked of her!" Margot broke in rudely. I never ceased to be astonished at how violent even the most normally well-behaved people could be when talking to their mothers. Margot would never have spoken that way to anyone else. She was like a teen-ager who had been told she couldn't go to the movies. "Ted and Jim simply presented you with a *fait accompli*. You made the best of it, I grant, but you weren't really much interested."

"Margot!" I protested.

"Well, she wasn't, Chris! She's always cared for the

171 ]

masses, never the individuals. She accepted Ted's and Jim's second wives as complacently as she did their first. And I'm sure she would accept Chuck once we were married. That's not what I'm worried about."

"It seems to me you're rather difficult to satisfy, my child," Polly intervened. "You want me to be enthusiastic about divorce. Well, I'm not enthusiastic about divorce, and I won't pretend to be. I think people should work on their marriages. I know something about that. Your father was not the easiest man in the world to live with." Here, rather engagingly, she reached over to give my hand a little pat. "We are telling you all our secrets, Chris!"

"But your problems were all solved by Father's death!"

It told worlds of how much Polly had learned to take from her children that this retort should not have brought even a faint pink to her cheeks. Margot was the one who flushed. I now began to realize how desperately upset she was. There was no question about it: this tense, humorless girl was very much in love, and it did not make her any more attractive. Polly now tried to be helpful.

"Perhaps you'd better tell me, my dear, just what it is you want me to do."

"It's very simple. I want you to talk to Mrs. Bannard and persuade her to be as tolerant as you are."

"Talk to Justine? I'd never dream of it!"

"Oh, Mother, won't you ever do *anything* for me?"

"What do you mean, child? What haven't I done for you?"

"Have *I* raised any objection while you dish out my inheritance to those loons in Moral Rearmament? Have I once reproached you?"

"No, you haven't, I'll admit that. You're not like your brothers, although I almost prefer their vociferous opposition to your contemptuous neutrality. Anyway, the money I give away is all my own. I've never touched a penny of the Wadsworth trusts."

"That's because you can't!"

"Your tone is unkind, dear. Those trusts one day will go to you and your brothers. What's mine I'm free to dispose of as I think best for all concerned. Don't you agree, Chris?"

"People are always going to differ about that, Polly. I happen to believe that one should hand on inherited money to one's descendants. But there's no law, moral or otherwise, that says that."

"Well, *my* moral law tells me that money given to God's cause will do more for my children than high living!"

"Oh, Mother! When did I live high?"

"Please, both of you, this topic isn't going to get us anywhere," I protested. "Polly, let me put it this way. We live in a day when, whether you like it or not, practically everyone who wants to divorce and remarry ultimately succeeds in doing so. So why prolong the agony? Let's get it over with as quickly and quietly as possible. Justine Bannard has immense influence with her daughter-in-law. If you go to her and tell her that, as is obviously the case, you dislike the whole business as much as she does, but that you believe it's in everyone's interest to come to a solution . . ."

"But I'm not at all sure I do!" Polly interrupted excitedly. "Why is it in Jill's interest to lose her husband?"

"A husband who'll hate her?"

"He might change. That has been known."

"Mother, he won't change. He's not like Daddy!"

173 ]

"He changed from Jill to you."

"Well, if he sticks with me for twenty years, I'll be perfectly satisfied!"

"It may be as you both say," Polly remarked after a pause, and I noted the new sad high note in her tone. "And it may be that you, Margot, and Chuck and Jill will work this thing out in what is called a civilized way. But it is asking too much of me to urge a wronged wife to surrender her rights."

"Oh, Mother, what terms! A 'wronged' wife? A 'surrender'?"

"I use my terms advisedly, child."

As she spoke she gained confidence, and I realized with a sinking heart that I was witnessing the metamorphosis of Polly Travers the woman into Polly Travers the orator. Ordinarily this happened only when she rose at a banquet to the tinkle of spoons on glasses and reached out a hand to approach the amplifier, like a crucifix, to her lips. But now, our questions had had the effect of an audience on her. Margot and I had only ourselves to blame for losing her mother as an ally.

"There have been things in my life of which you aren't aware, Margot," she continued serenely. "I know what it is to be a loyal wife who is snubbed and scorned for trying to serve her lord and master. Your father would have left me for a certain Mrs. Donaldson had he not awakened to the fact that the widow's jointure that she would have sacrificed on a second marriage was far greater than anything *he* had to bring her . . ."

"Oh, Mother, everyone knew about Mrs. Donaldson. Please keep your voice down!"

"Why should I, if everyone knows about it? I have been accustomed to humiliation from childhood. I have been taught by masters. My parents used to sneer at Polly and her *pauvres*. My husband protested that I never took my proper position in society. My own children jeered at my politics and my faith."

"Mother, you're being absurd."

"Can you deny, Margot, that you don't all laugh at me?"

"Oh, we may laugh, but in a friendly way. A loving way."

"None of you has ever loved me!" Polly exclaimed with sudden heat. Yet her tone was not bitter; it was exalted. "I have had to make my own way, my own life. Perhaps all of us do. I do not complain. But when I see a poor woman in the position that *I* was in, despised and rejected, I know that I am not going to utter one word or lift one finger to encourage those who are despising and rejecting her! Not even if my own daughter's happiness is at stake!"

I could see by Margot's dropped jaw that she knew the cause was lost. "And where is that daughter to go for happiness?"

"You could pray, my child. Others in trouble have found that the way."

Margot at this simply got up and quit the table. Polly and I silently watched her at the checkroom counter, getting her coat. Then she was gone. As we turned without appetite to our lunch, Polly tried to proselytize me for Moral Rearmament. She must have been desperate for converts.

———

Unfortunately for her daughter and Chuck, Polly did not confine her espousal of Jill Bannard's cause to a discreet silence, but openly championed it at a session of the Book Class itself. Mother related to me the remarkable circumstance.

"I don't know when we've seen anything like it. Polly was very silent during the soup, when we have our general discussion. But she had that impassioned look that, as we all know, generally precedes one of her public utterances. Just before we were to start on the book of the day, she announced that she had something to tell us. She proceeded to explain that we were a small, tight group and that it would be idle to pretend that we did not know about Margot and Chuck. And then, soaring above the astonished silence of the table and fixing her eyes on Justine, who bent hers fixedly on her plate, she proclaimed her abiding faith in the marriage vow! She told us that she was praying that her daughter would be given the grace to cease interfering with the domestic tranquillity of the Charles Bannards. Well! None of us knew where to look. Until Justine, in a flat voice, said: 'Thank you, Polly. I'm sure that was a difficult thing to say. And now, shall we get on to the book?'"

"Was she furious with Polly?"

"It's hard to say. Justine is a very private person. She's not one to air her problems at Book Class. But I suspect she may welcome any allies in this fight."

"And the whole Class is behind her?"

"Including your mother, darling. Who doesn't in the least approve of your mixing yourself up with Chuck and that nasty little Margot Travers!"

"A woman in love is always nasty — if she's frustrated."

"Well, what business does she have being in love with a married man?"

"I won't defend her. Chuck is my only concern in this business."

"Then tell him to give her up! But why do I talk to you? I can leave *that* to Justine."

What Mother meant by this dark hint I discovered the next morning, when my secretary announced Mrs. Bannard on the telephone.

"Good morning, Christopher," came the clear, cool tones. They were not accusatory, merely declarative. "I know what a busy man you are, and I'll take only a minute of your time. I wish you, as Chuck's confidant, to hear what I have to say to him in relation to you-know-what. He's coming to me at six. Can you be here?"

"On the dot, ma'am."

I had to break an engagement, but that was nothing. Justine Bannard was not a person to waste one's time. When I went to her house at the appointed hour I was ushered into a small dark library, where there was no sign of tea or other libation. Justine was seated at a bare table on which she had folded her hands. Chuck, his back to me, stood by a gauze-curtained window, looking out at nothing and putting me in mind of Max Beerbohm's famed cartoon "The rare, the rather awful visits of Albert Edward, Prince of Wales, to Windsor Castle." But Justine's voice, when she spoke, was almost friendly.

"I shan't beat about the bush, boys. I'm going to put my cards on the table. This is not a bargaining session; I'm not here to listen to arguments. I have made up my mind what I shall do, and I shall do it. So here it is. If Chuck leaves Jill and marries Margot Travers, I shall change my will, substituting Jill's name for his in every place where his occurs.

Everything else will remain the same. I shall hope that Chuck and I will still be on affectionate terms, and I shall make every effort to get on with his new wife. But Jill will be my legal child insofar as all property arrangements are concerned. Is that clear, Christopher? You are a witness."

"Crystal clear, ma'am. Let me ask you just one thing."

"A question, yes. An argument, no."

"This is a question. Supposing Jill were to consent to a divorce. Would your position be the same?"

"Precisely the same. For I should know she had done it only because she had been badgered into it."

"And any children that Chuck and Margot might have — what of them?"

Justine smiled. Chuck, who still had his back to us, showed his impatience with a gesture of an arm. "You should have been a lawyer, Christopher. I don't say that I shouldn't make some provision for a new grandchild, but Jill would still have Chuck's share of my estate."

If my reader will now glance back at the "short story" that I wrote about Justine and Amelie Buck, he may decide that my fiction was not so fictional.

Chuck now turned around, looking like a surly little boy. "I thought you cared about me, Ma."

"People have different ways of showing how they care."

"They certainly do. Well, Chris, shall we go? I think I'll let you buy me a drink."

It interested me that he knew his mother well enough to see that argument was hopeless. At the bar to which we repaired the only hope that I could think of offering him was that Justine, who seemed to be made of leather, would probably survive him, so that her will might not really matter to him in the end, but I decided that this was worse than nothing. Besides, it wasn't necessary. He had given Margot up. Chuck could not face a future stripped of what he deemed the inalienable right of his inheritance. The males of my generation and group were far more conservative than the females. Margot would have gladly given up the world for love; she wouldn't have thought twice about it. But the male who was not a moneymaker (and Chuck, though he earned a decent living, was far from opulent) had a profound respect for the produce of his more fruitful male ancestors. He knew, deep down, that inherited wealth was what gave him his "balls," and that it would do him little good to elope with Margot if he left those circular objects behind. He talked that night much more about his mother than he did about Margot. It seemed to give him consolation to describe her as a bitch.

Was Justine justified in her stand? Perhaps, if judged by subsequent events. Chuck and Jill remained married, just as tepidly as before, but no more so, at least as far as a dinner guest could tell. Jill was too wise, or perhaps too indifferent, to allow old resentments to show. And Margot, who three years later married a divorced man, also a dozen years older than herself, also a stockbroker, has been reputed to be a bit of a shrew. But who knows? Mated to Chuck, she might have been a paragon of wives. Her character may have been permanently blighted by her defeat by the Book Class.

Polly Travers herself incurred the united condemnation of that entity when she instituted a suit to break one of the Wadsworth trusts so that she could hand over the principal to Moral Rearmament. This attempt to deprive her descendants of what the Class regarded as their God-given due could not be approved, even if God was the proposed beneficiary. Justine herself would never have tampered with a family trust, even to preserve a son's marriage. *Some* things had to be sacred! When Polly lost her suit, no comment was made by the other members, but when she had the gall to appeal to the table for sympathy against this "unjust decision," she received such a rebuff that she resigned from the Class, the only member in its long history to do so. But by this time she had become such a fanatic that she was little missed.

## 13

THERE WAS one member of the Book Class whom I did not really get to know until 1964, when she was in her mid-seventies — their "European representative," the Marquise de Terrasson, who lived the year round in a moldering château in Burgundy and had not attended a meeting of the Class in decades. She had been born Genevieve Torrance, of the New York department store family, and in the days of her prosperity she had crossed the Atlantic every winter to bring to at least one meeting a vividly appreciated international flavor. I can remember how much they had all made of their one titled member and how often "darling Genevieve" was quoted to sustain their opinions on Gallic art or politics. This may seem odd in view of the more splendid European connections of some of the Class, but a shared youth has a tenacious appeal, and Genevieve, remembered as a young and pretty marquise, retained a glamour that she might not have had, encountered later in their lives.

After the marquis's death and the foundering of Torrance's in the Great Depression, the widow had had to pull in her horns. The *hôtel* in Paris and the villa at Cannes were sold, and Genevieve had retired to the ancestral hold in Bligny-sur-Ouche, where she lived, according to the report of those members who looked her up, in frugal and patient simplicity, totally absorbed in her immediate environment and quite detached from Yankee memories. Yet all agreed that she still welcomed visitors, and Mother and I on a spring motor trip to France directed our wheels towards Dijon.

I should say a word about that trip. Mother and I had never been more congenial. She was now a vigorous and comely seventy-four; Father was long gone, and Manny and Eleanor too preoccupied with their own lives and families to need much of her time and attention. To tell the truth, Mother was undergoing the kind of disillusionment that I have frequently observed in parents as their offspring pass into middle age. With the loss of the glow of youth and the advent of a crabby self-obsession, the latter become less beguiling, and their unconcealed preference for their own usually badly brought-up issue is bound to increase the disenchantment. An unmarried child, on the other hand, is less apt to regard a parent as a mere source of financial assistance. I treated Mother as a human being, and in France, with nothing in the immediate foreground to remind her of domestic duties that she might conceivably be neglecting, we got on splendidly. Mother, indeed, waxed almost aesthetic in her appreciation of cathedrals and museums. She seemed released from a philistine past.

As we approached Dijon on the auto route, she described to me our hostess-to-be.

"Genevieve lives in a different world — in what used to be called *vieille France* — cold, dreary châteaux hidden away in the provinces, where you see only cousins of cousins and complain that the Comte de Paris is an Orléans."

"And if there are six people for tea, six cookies?"

"No, five. The hostess doesn't take one. That world was pretty well gone even when she married Amaury in nineteen twelve. There can't be more than a few bones of it left now."

"Where there's a will to resurrect it, I suppose there's a way. I am told that, up the Hudson, there are families that still refer to Robert Livingston as 'the chancellor.' But did the Faubourg Saint-Germain take her in? She didn't smell too much of the department store?"

"Those people don't distinguish between Americans. So long as there's money, it doesn't matter where it came from. The only thing they minded was when it went. Genevieve herself was rather relieved, I imagine. It wasn't there anymore to remind her of her low origin!"

"She was ashamed of being a Torrance?"

"Only when she remembered it. I think for the most part she repressed the idea. Like Millie Grey, who seems literally to have forgotten that she's Jewish."

"Isn't that rather a feat when your father was Jacob Wise?"

"You would think so. But Millie's done it. And wait till you meet Genevieve. When I see her, I feel that somehow I didn't know her before she was a marquise."

"You're describing a psychopathic snob."

"And yet the funny thing is that she isn't — not really. When we were young, she had no idea of social stratifications. You could never have explained to her, for example, the difference between a Torrance, still a bit smelling of retail, and, say, a . . ."

"A Gallatin," I supplied maliciously.

"All right, a Gallatin," Mother affirmed proudly. "Genevieve was somehow above those things. She was always teaching poetry to stenographers in night class or doing something noble about soup kitchens. Questions of birth and rank didn't exist for her until she came over here."

"What was her husband like?"

"Amaury? A typical French husband of that *monde*. Utterly charming, utterly unfaithful. He spent most of the money that her brothers didn't lose and died scandalously in a *maison de passe*. There are two daughters, both married appropriately, and a rather seedy bachelor son, who lives at home. He'll probably try to borrow money from you."

"Thanks for the warning." We were now approaching the Château de Terrasson.

It was a long white rectangular Louis XV edifice, framed by four turreted stone towers, sole relics of the medieval castle that had once defended and no doubt exploited the village of Bligny-sur-Ouche.

"Madame la Marquise," we were told by the ancient crone who came at last to the door, was at market, so we had time, after settling in our rooms, to examine the ground floor of the château. The parlor was a large handsome white chamber with french windows opening on a sad little terrace with a fine view of the forest beyond. The furniture was a rather worn Louis XVI that needed refurbishing; it was obvious that no money had been spent on the place in years. Yet everything was clean. If the old crone did the dusting and polishing, Madame certainly got her money's worth.

"Why are the portraits so bad?" Mother was standing before a likeness of Queen Marie Leczinska that might have been done by a demoiselle de Terrasson.

"Because Napoleon did away with primogeniture. When the heir had to divvy up his inheritance with half a dozen brothers and sisters, the only way he could keep the château was by giving them the heirlooms. So unless he had the luck to have married a Rothschild or a Gould, he had to satisfy himself with bad copies of what his siblings hauled away."

"And that's why the English still have treasure houses? Because the girls get nothing? It's fortunate for me my father wasn't a lord."

"Is it? Daddy would never have married you."

"Chris! You ought to have your mouth washed out with soap!"

I saw that I had gone too far. The remarkable intimacy of our trip had made me push my luck. I was even considering an apology when we heard from the hallway the high, clear, bell-like tones of a Book Class member.

"Cornelia darling! You're here, and I've kept you waiting. How shameful!"

But if Genevieve de Terrasson sounded like a classmate, she certainly did not look like one. The lively but rather dumpy little lady who now bustled into the parlor was clad in a brown potato sack of a dress that matched her tousled strawlike hair. Yet there was a remnant of prettiness in her round, smooth, unpowdered face and large yellow-brown eyes.

"And this is Christopher! Good heavens, it must be twenty years. What a fine fellow he's become!"

It seemed clear enough to me that I was an unlikely representative of the class that Madame de Terrasson would regard as fine fellows, yet there was no denying the force of her good will. Now she was actually telling me about an article that she had read about my work in *House and Garden*.

"I was so proud to think I was an old friend of your mother's! My, my, what an imagination it must take to dream up all those beautiful rooms! Over here we're too

185 ]

used to accepting passively what we inherit. We get lazy, I fear. It's good to have someone like your son to keep us up to snuff, isn't it, Cornelia?"

I was softened to the point of offering her an uncharacteristic piece of flattery. "You have a fine room here, ma'am."

"You must call me Genevieve. Justine Bannard was here last month, and she said that you called all the Book Class by their Christian names. I don't want to be the one exception — just because I have a handle to my name!"

"Very well, Genevieve."

At lunch, which was simple but adequate, we met her son, Armand, an ugly, sallow, emaciated creature of some fifty years whose fixed smile of supposed welcome somehow managed to be insulting. Rarely have I so instantly taken a dislike to a man. During the meal Genevieve asked Mother about the books discussed at last year's meetings, none of which, it appeared, she had read.

"But then it's impossible to run this old place and find much time to read," she explained. "Still, I don't want you to think I've lost my taste for literature. Actually, I have embarked on a little project of my own."

"You're writing your memoirs!" Mother exclaimed. "Justine told us."

"Well, it's really just an experiment. I thought maybe it was time to set down a few of the things I've been privileged to see. It's a tiny something I can do for the nation that's been so good to me." Here she turned her benign gaze on me. "France is a wonderful country to live in, Christopher. If you don't too much mind being occupied by nasty Germans every so often."

"Maman considers herself a latter-day Madame de Sévigné!"

Armand exclaimed in a mocking tone. "Our little château will become a Mecca, like George Sand's villa at Nogent!"

"Oh, Armand, you mustn't be silly!" his mother protested, blushing as if she had received a compliment.

"The story of the Terrassons will have waited all these years for an American viewpoint!" her son continued with a cackle.

"And why not?" I demanded indignantly. I turned abruptly to my hostess. "I have written a few things myself, Genevieve, and I number some publishers among my good friends. I should be greatly honored if you would allow me to read what you've written. I might be of some help."

"Well, you're very dear, and I may impose on you to glance at a few pages," Genevieve replied, looking apprehensively at her son.

That very night I found a half-dozen short chapters, penned in a large, legible lady's hand, piled neatly on the table by my bedside, with a note from my hostess informing me that a candid judgment would be deeply appreciated.

It was the first of three parts, and was called "Marriage." A note at the end promised that the next two installments would be entitled "Between the Wars" and "A Château in Burgundy in the Occupation." As Genevieve was reputed to have concealed Allied pilots in her barn while German officers occupied the château, the last part seemed to offer exciting possibilities.

My hopes, however, were dashed as I perused the initial sketch. It was not that Genevieve could not write; she had a clear, firm, simple style that carried her reader pleasantly enough from one sentence to the next. What was wrong was the point of view. It was difficult to realize that the manuscript in my hands had been written when the twentieth century was three-quarters spent. The author might have been a pupil of Chateaubriand's.

Amaury de Terrasson emerged from his wife's pages as a model husband, a loving father, a humane landlord and, finally, as a gallant soldier. Here is how Genevieve described her father's consent to her engagement:

> Papa was naturally upset that I should marry away from my native land. He had strong family feeling, and when my two brothers married he expected their wives to occupy the two smaller red brick residences that he had erected on either side of his own on Forty-eighth Street. But when he came to know Amaury, he quickly understood what an exciting challenge it might be for an American girl to take her place in an older, perhaps even a wiser order of civilization.

When I thought of the scene that must have taken place between the greedy, mortgaged nobleman of the Côte d'Or and the harassed department store owner, driven, no doubt, by a socially ambitious wife, I could only rub my eyes at Genevieve's naïveté.

The following morning after breakfast I found my hostess in the vegetable garden, arrayed in an old gray mantle. She rose from her squatting position when she saw me coming, a pair of small shears in one hand, a bunch of lettuce leaves in the other.

"What is the judgment?" she asked in a pleasant tone. "Shall I stuff it in the fire?"

"By no means. It reads very well. But tell me something. Did your husband have no faults?"

Her smile was of a serenity. "None. Why?"

"Couldn't you lend him a few? Your readers will want some spots."

"I'm afraid I shall have to disappoint them."

"But will there be some people with faults in the rest of the book?"

"Oh, dear boy! Wait till I get to the Germans!"

"I suppose that may help." I searched my mind for something that might give life to her memoir. "It strikes me that you rather scant your American background. There's almost nothing about your childhood or Torrance's Store."

She seemed to give this some surprised thought. "It may seem funny to you, but I've been French so long that it's hard for me to realize I wasn't always so."

"And yet it is commonly said that our most vivid years are those of childhood."

"It wasn't true of mine."

"Don't be offended at my next suggestion. Readers today expect to be taken behind the scenes. They will certainly be interested in the difference between American and French marriage customs. For example, a French marquis would certainly have expected a dowry, and your father might well have thought a son-in-law ought to support his daughter. How were those two viewpoints reconciled?"

Genevieve burst into a cheerful laugh. "But, my dear Christopher, I haven't the faintest idea! Amaury and I were like babes in the woods where those matters were concerned. We left them all to the lawyers!"

The late marquis's sister, the Comtesse de Bourbon-Busset, also a widow, came over for lunch on the first Sunday of our visit. She was a great hawk of a woman, with dyed raven hair, considerably more worldly than Genevieve, and very direct and down-to-earth. I was told that she had little money, but was a welcome visitor at many great households and was spending a week at the Château de Sully.

"If you're looking for a job, Mr. Gates," she announced to me in crisp English, "there are plenty of places in this neighborhood that could do with a new look. Only I can't imagine what they'd pay you with."

"I'm on vacation, thank you, Comtesse. Besides, I'm tired of done-up rooms. I love empty halls."

"If that's what you want, we can give you a feast!"

"Genevieve tells me the Bussets belong to a branch of the Bourbons older than the Pretender's," I said, changing the subject rather abruptly, for I liked to discuss my trade only with professionals. "Is that so? She says that if Louis the Eleventh hadn't refused to recognize the marriage of one of your ancestors, they'd have succeeded to the throne ahead of Henry of Navarre."

I have learned in Europe that with titled folk it is always acceptable to talk of their ancestry — despite the fashionable requirement that they pretend to pooh-pooh it — provided one is serious.

"Well, it doesn't do us much good now, does it?" Madame de Busset replied, snapping her tinted eyelids. "Genevieve's a great one for that kind of thing. Only I'm sure she didn't use the term 'Pretender.'"

"No, that was mine. She's more of a Royalist than the Comte de Paris. She calls him Henri the Sixth. Did you know she was writing her memoirs?"

"Oh, yes." As with her nephew, it immediately struck me that she was not pleased. "Has she let you read them? I have not been so honored."

"Only a few pages. But I can assure you that you have nothing to worry about."

She laughed in surprise. "My dear young man, why on earth should I worry?"

"We always do at home if anyone writes a book. We're afraid they're going to rattle the skeletons in the closet. But you're quite safe. I gather you don't have any. Everyone in Madame de Terrasson's pages is pure as pure."

"How dull. Who will read it then?"

"I can't imagine. There used to be an American audience for memoirs of heiresses who married titles, but it's much diminished."

"So have the heiresses. And so have the titles."

We moved to another subject, and I was sorry that I had said what I had. Why should Madame de Busset object to her sister-in-law's harmless manuscript? Perhaps she was afraid that Genevieve would make the family ridiculous with her social pretensions. It may have been this that was responsible for a noticeably tart remark that she made later, during that same meal. Genevieve had been speaking of one of her granddaughters, who had recently become engaged to a young man in the advertising business whose name, Pierre Boulanger, hardly suggested a connection that would have entitled his wife to a *tabouret* in the court of the Sun King.

"He's a perfect darling, and I think Suzanne is going to be very happy. Of course, he isn't exactly in the Almanach de Gotha. But perhaps our old stock will benefit with a little mixing."

"I don't know that we Terrassons are such old stock, Genevieve," her sister-in-law retorted. "I know that *my* mother-in-law made me feel like a Johnny-come-lately when I joined the Busset tribe. But no doubt, across the Atlantic, your forebears go back to the forest primeval."

I remembered now what Mother had said about Millie Grey forgetting that she was Jewish. When I glanced at Genevieve, I noted that nothing in the blandness of her expression or in the misty kindness with which she surveyed her critical relative indicated that the latter's barb had struck home.

"I suppose we may have some Indian blood," Genevieve murmured vaguely. "I really don't know."

Later that night, when I went to Mother's room to bid her good night, she asked me triumphantly whether I had noticed Genevieve's reaction.

"You see, I was right, Chris! She actually believes she's French and that her family-in-law are all perfect. I remember, years ago, when your father and I were dining with Genevieve and Amaury in Paris, and Madame de Busset was there, that the most embarrassing thing happened. Amaury, who could be very strict about other people's morals, had been holding forth on some cousin who had left his wife for a *cocotte*, when his sister — just the way she did tonight — got fed up. Her cool tones rang down the table: 'It seems to me, *mon frère*, that you take a pretty high tone for a man who has been the hero of two stinking society scandals!' Well, nobody knew where to look, except Genevieve, who immediately protested that Amaury had been the victim of vicious lies! And she *believed* it, God bless her. I think she even believed that Amaury went to that brothel the night he died to warn a friend that his wife was having him followed by a detective!"

Mother was sitting up in bed in a red wrapper, her hair in curlers. Her enjoyment of her own story made her seem almost girlish.

"Your friend Genevieve seems to have created a world as surely as Jehovah did in Genesis."

"Your father got an enormous kick out of Madame de

Busset's boldness. 'I admire that woman,' he told me afterwards. 'We could use her in Personnel at the bank.' "

In bed that night I thought of Father deriving the same amusement from Madame de Busset's candor that I had, and it made me feel closer to him than I had ever remembered feeling. Had he lived a bit longer, had I been less touchy — might we have been friends?

The next morning, after Genevieve had gone to her garden and while Mother was breakfasting in bed, I found myself alone in the dining room with Armand.

"I gather you have been reading the famous memoirs," he observed with his odiously smiling sneer.

"And enjoying them immensely," I retorted stoutly.

"Isn't that nice? Do you think Maman will find a publisher?"

"I should certainly think so," I affirmed, determined not to give him the answer he obviously wanted.

"And that being the case, could she look to a large sale?"

"I shouldn't be surprised if she sold it to the movies!"

The idea of a profit seemed for a moment to mitigate his dismay. But then he cackled. "You're joking, of course."

"Tell me, Armand. What is it that you don't like about your mother's memoirs? It seems to me they're entirely laudatory about the family."

"Well, you know we have our pride," he said, drawing himself up with unexpected loftiness. "I don't think anyone in our family has ever published a book."

"Perhaps then it's time."

"Would *your* mother write a book about relatives?"

I considered this. "I really don't know. But if she did, I should certainly have no objection."

"I suppose it's impossible for you to put yourself in the position of an old Burgundian family."

"Mother for mother, however, I guess we can swap. I'll back the Gallatins against the Torrances any day!"

But nothing would stop him from fawning.

"My sisters and I would be eternally obliged to you if you could discourage Maman in her project."

Genevieve came in from the garden at this moment, and the conversation had to end. But I was determined now to get to the bottom of Armand's reiterated objections to his mother's harmless publication, and I decided to consult Madame de Busset directly. Why should poor Genevieve's innocuous pastime fall before the snobbishness and contempt of a family that had done nothing but exploit her? I was quite boiling with indignation by the time I saw her sister-in-law.

Madame de Busset had invited me to drive over to see Sully any time during her visit there, and so, while Mother and Genevieve were visiting one of the latter's innumerable cousins-in-law, I went to the great palace of Henri IV's minister. Madame de Busset gave me a tour of the château and grounds — the house party had gone to Tournus for the day — and we strolled afterwards in the great flat garden beyond the moat.

"You have something on your mind, Monsieur Gates," my guide told me at last, "besides seventeenth-century architecture. Let us sit down and discuss it."

"You are very perceptive!" We seated ourselves on a marble bench. "It is about your sister-in-law's memoirs. Why does her son not wish her to publish them?"

"Oh, he's told you that, has he?"

"He made it very plain. He purports to dread the publicity. This seems to me curious in a man who turns at once in any newspaper to the society page."

"*You* are the one who is perceptive, *mon ami*. Let us put it that Armand hates certain kinds of publicity."

"But from what I've read of Genevieve's memoirs, he has nothing whatever to fear! On the contrary, everything in them is *couleur de rose*. The noblest of old families, the happiest of marriages, the gallantest of war records . . ."

"It makes us just a bit ridiculous, don't you think?"

"But everyone knows memoirs are written like that. It's a tradition. Oh, yes, Cecil Beaton spoofed it in *My Royal Past*, but that only proved how widespread it is."

"Well, I don't so much mind the lineage nonsense, or even the happy marriages. But I cannot help balking at the gallant war records."

"I thought the marquis was a hero in the first war! I thought that at least was true."

"Oh, Amaury did his bit, I grant. It was, as Mr. Churchill would have put it, his finest hour. Perhaps his only fine one. No, in *that* war we were very well. But the last one . . . *c'est une autre histoire. Ecoutez, mon ami*, I don't constitute myself a judge in these matters. France went through hell, and some of us found ourselves at home there. There was the underground, of course, and many were in it. But not all, though all now claim it. To hear the chatter in Paris today, you would think there had been nobody *above*ground."

"You mean that in your family there were . . . collaborationists?"

"My husband was in the underground. One of my nephews was shot by the Boches. I still call them that, yes! And Genevieve herself risked her life doing some of the things she did. But Armand and Pierre, who married Genevieve's older daughter, were in the black market and perhaps worse. Perhaps considerably worse."

"You amaze me!"

"You will not find a family in France, monsieur, where the problem does not exist. Anyway, it is over. Armand was acquitted by one of our courts of *épuration*, though there were those who hinted at doctored evidence. But most people have now decided to look the other way. That is, so long as a suspect party doesn't go around crowing that he's the Chevalier Bayard!"

"Which would be the effect of Genevieve's book? I see. Do you suppose she has any supposition of what went on?"

Madame de Busset's shrug rippled her shoulders like a billow. "Who knows what Genevieve supposes? I've long given up trying to make it out. I used to think it was because she was American — forgive me — but now I see it must be just her. Would your mother be capable of such self-delusion? Surely not."

"Not to the same extent, anyway."

"It's not, then, a characteristic of the famous Book Class that Genevieve is always talking about?"

"Does she always talk about it? Perhaps self-delusion *is* their danger!"

"Certainly, it's not yours, *mon ami*. Will you try, then, to discourage Genevieve from her proposed publication?"

"No!" I was surprised at the violence of my sudden resolution. "But you needn't worry. She's never going to find a publisher — her memoirs are much too flat — and I gather there's not enough money around to pay for vanity printing. But I want Armand to sweat it out. I think that may be a small piece of the punishment he deserves!"

Madame de Busset chuckled. "I wish you lived over here, Monsieur Gates. I think you and I might be friends."

"I come to Paris enough to make that possible. Let me take you up on it! And in the meantime Genevieve will have the fun of finishing her book. There's something really rather noble about it, you know. Look what your family has done to her. They married her for her money and humiliated her. Her own son betrayed her highest ideals. And how did she respond to this treatment? By stubbornly erecting a temple of beauty in her mind, by placing in it a golden image and worshipping it. Who said there's no money for vanity printing? Maybe *I* shall pay for a private publication of her book! Just in New York, and in English — you need have no fear of repercussions over here. I wonder whether, as a psychological document, it wouldn't be worth it!"

Madame de Busset grunted as she rose from the bench. "Well, you can admire that sort of thing, if you like, my clever young man. But I'm too much of a realist. And who, I'd like to know, will read your expensive undertaking?"

"The one audience that will appreciate it. The Book Class!"

"Oh, the Book Class," she muttered as she turned back to the château. "I guess you're right. Armand will have nothing to fear."

## 14

I NOTE in reading over these pages that I imply that I ultimately called all members of the Book Class by their Christian names. But the one member with whom I had never taken this liberty was Mrs. Erskine. She is also, in 1980 as I write these lines, the sole survivor of the group, or at least the only one I can still see. Genevieve de Terrasson is alive, but she never leaves her bedroom in her Burgundian château, and Polly Travers is in a nursing home, where she is said to deliver dotty sermons to the attendants. The rest are all dead.

But Maud Erskine is going strong at ninety-three. Being a bit older than the others, she was not one of the founding debutante members. She was not elected until the suicide of Leila Lee, by which time, a widow, she had come back to New York after a life in the diplomatic service. She had, however, known the Class longer than that, having grown up more or less in their world, though born with the unlikely surname of Alamanza. Her father, an Argentinian adventurer seeking money in marriage, had disappeared after discovering that the Hudson River bride with whom he had eloped did not have enough of it, and Maud, sole fruit of this unhappy union, had been reared, after her broken-hearted mother's early demise, by her maternal grandmother, Mrs. Schuyler Kip, in the genteel poverty of an ancient Rhinebeck clan.

Mother used to tell me pathetic stories of Maud Alamanza's girlhood. The grandmother had evidently determined that nothing was going to matter about poor Maud — her tallness, her gauntness, her plainness, her poverty — so long as the Alamanza streak in her was rigidly suppressed. The old lady had too strict a regard for the rights of blood to change the girl's name, but certainly nothing, according to Mother, could less have suggested castanets and raven ringlets than the homely puritan features and dull watery orbs of Alamanza's daughter. Maud had grown up a solitary child in Mrs. Kip's somber household; she had meekly accepted the rigors of a parsimonious introduction to society, and had then embraced, with apparent resignation, the duties of nurse-companion to her ancient ancestress. But she had a shock in store for those who pitied her. Shortly after the old lady's death, Maud, aged thirty, had astonished society by announcing her engagement to Craig Erskine!

It had been a great match financially. Craig's father, as a young man, had had the good fortune to make a small loan to the also young John D. Rockefeller, secured by shares in an oil venture. And I suppose, at least from the bride's point of view, it had been a sufficiently great match diplomatically. "Poor Maud" had ultimately become the consort of our Minister to Honduras. But I remembered Mr. Erskine most unfavorably from my childhood at one of my parents' weekends, a stout, gray, choleric gentleman who, when not holding forth fussily, though perhaps knowledgeably, on French eighteenth-century bibelots, was declaiming noisily, even rather alarmingly, over some imagined slight to his person or fault in service. Why in God's name had he married Maud?

When I called her on the telephone, last fall, to ask her, as my sole living source of information, whether I could talk to her about the Book Class, she professed herself amused at the idea. She concluded in her low, solemn voice, "We are the survivors, Christopher. *We* can talk."

It struck me that she might mean what she said. If she was obviously a woman of discretion and dignity, she was also, I divined, a person who was afraid of nothing, who, once she had decided that it was the right thing to do, would speak out and let the chips fall. I decided to tell her of my project.

"I have written some chapters about your classmates. Would you care to read them?"

"Are they typed? My eyes are not too good."

"Of course they're typed."

"And have you a copy? I'd hate to be responsible for the only one."

"Mrs. Erskine, we live in the age of duplication! You can throw your copy in the trash can when you finish it. Only, I hope you'll preserve your opinion of it so that I may have the benefit."

"You won't mind if I don't like it?"

"I don't expect you to like it."

"Very well then. On those conditions. Mail it to me. I'll read it before we meet."

Age had mitigated Maud Erskine's homeliness, and extreme old age had even made her into a kind of impressive monument. Her long brown face, her long arms and purple veins, her gray straggly hair, still mixed with auburn, her huge staring hazel eyes, the shapeless black of her dress, put me in mind of some large, dark, blinking lizard, faintly panting on a rock in the sun. She had never affected jewels or fine clothes, and she was certainly not going to start now. She lived mostly up the Hudson in the old Kip mansion, but when she came to town she occupied the gray French *hôtel* designed for her husband by Ogden Codman on East Seventy-third Street. Here, with one old maid and I suppose a janitor, she camped out amid elegant divans and bergères draped in summer covers, under Lancrets and Hubert Roberts that needed cleaning. Nothing could have more impressed me both with her wealth and her indifference to it than that she should have kept such valuable real estate for such casual use.

When I came to make my call, I stood for a full five minutes in the quiet vestibule, relentlessly pressing the bell. I knew that Agnes was partly deaf and almost as old as her mistress. Eventually the door opened a crack on a chain.

"Who is it?" came Maud's deep voice.

"It's me, Mrs. Erskine."

The chain was removed, and I followed my hostess's tall, broad, retreating back up the marble curving stairway to the parlor. "What happened to Agnes?" I asked.

"What do you think happened to Agnes?" she retorted without turning. "The service was last Friday."

"Oh, I'm sorry."

"Don't be sorry. It was high time. All my friends have got their passports. Only mine seems to be held up."

"As I hope it will continue to be."

"Don't hope, Christopher. But here we are." On a table by the white covered sofa in the dim parlor was a kitchen tray with two crude china cups and a pot. "I made you some tea myself."

It was typical of Maud that we should have our plain brew in servants' dishes surrounded by a million dollars worth of art. How Craig Erskine would have stared! But he was long dead. There was no cream, but she provided a piece of lemon. I noted on the little stand by my chair a small leather-bound volume with three castles in the stamped coat of arms.

"From the library of Madame de Pompadour," I observed, picking it up to admire it.

"Is that what it is? Do you suppose she ever read it?"

"She may have." I turned it to read the title on the spine. "Voltaire! Then she definitely did."

Maud grunted. "A bluestocking as well as a whore. Would you like it? Take it."

"Mrs. Erskine, that little book is worth some three thousand dollars!"

"Really? You think I should keep it?"

"I think you should not give away things in this house so carelessly. You may find yourself with a surprising number of callers. And not all of the nicest sort."

Maud shrugged. "All right, my dear, I'll keep it. You're quite right about carelessness. Craig's things, after all, are my responsibility. But when I do my next will, shall I leave you the French books? Is that what you'd like?"

"I should adore it. But I shall have to survive you. That won't be so easy."

"Get on with you!" she said brusquely. "Let's talk about the Book Class."

For a while our discussion was desultory. Maud seemed content with the obvious: that Justine Bannard should have had an outlet to take care of her excess energy, that Georgia

Bristed should not have been so hipped on right-wing politics, that it was a pity Polly Travers had been such an ass. I tried to probe deeper.

"Would they have been happier had they been born fifty years later?"

"And had careers and divorces, you mean? Perhaps. It's hard to say. They were so much of their era that I can't visualize them out of it."

"And they approved of that era, didn't they? I mean, of the basic social structure?"

"Let's put it that none of them was a rebel. Yes, they accepted the status quo. But they accepted it critically. It was, after all, a men's status quo, and I think every one of them believed, deep down, that, given the opportunity, she could have made a better job of it."

"Even Mylo Jessup?"

"Oh, especially Mylo. She believed it was a woman's glory to manipulate a man without his knowing it. And without anyone's knowing it! It was supposed to be for his good, of course."

"I guess there's something in that," I mused. "Certainly Justine dominated Chester. And Georgia usually told old Pop where to get off. Even Mother held her own with Father. Do you suppose they secretly believed they were superior to men?"

Maud chuckled. "They thought they were superior to everybody! I said they weren't rebels. But they weren't pioneers, either. They accepted their world and their position in it. But they believed they had a duty to maintain that world and that position. They didn't even really believe that those things could endure without their effort. So they tried, in all good conscience."

"And did they succeed?"

"Well, you've seen what happened to their world. Gone!" Maud blew, as if extinguishing a match's flame. "When I look back on my girlhood, I might as well be looking at imperial Rome."

"You seem to imply that there was a difference between you and the rest of the Class. What was it?"

"All the difference between day and night! I had not been one of the original group. In those days I regarded them as so many princesses and myself as a kind of Cinderella for whom no coach was waiting."

"Yet you were a Kip and all that."

"I was a Kip, at least on the distaff side, but there was no 'all that,' Christopher. I was a Kip, period. My grandmother ground it into me, month after month, year after year, that having Kip blood was my sole distinction, but that it might be just distinction enough. And do you know something? I think it actually saved me!"

"You mean the blood?" I smiled. "Even on the distaff side?"

"No, I mean the *idea* of it. Grandma may have had method in her genealogical madness. For the idea, however ridiculous, that being a Kip — or even half a Kip — made up for ugliness and gaucheness and poverty may have pulled me through. You laugh, but I can remember a ball where I sat all evening with Grandma, without one man asking me to dance, except an elderly second cousin, and thinking that all those pretty girls might have been willing to trade half their fun for one drop of my old Kip blood!"

"Did you really?"

"Not really, but in fantasy. And fantasy may have been my armor. Fantasy may have been the scaffolding that sustained me until I could develop my own character. After that I could tear it down and throw it away. And be perfectly happy with the idea of Alamanza forebears who probably ran cat houses in Buenos Aires!"

"When did you meet Mr. Erskine?" I inquired, startled at such freedom with her family tree.

"My great *coup?* You want to come to that, do you? Everyone does. But I forget — did you know Craig?"

"Oh, yes. He banked with Daddy."

"And did you like him?"

"Very much."

"Liar!"

We both laughed. There was no point trying to fool her. I remembered Mr. Erskine standing in astonishment before a little Charpentier, *Le Déjeuner à la Chasse,* that Mother had inherited from an aunt and exclaiming, "But, Cornelia, I had no idea you had jewels like this!" I had thought him a fussy dilettantish old queen.

"Not many people really appreciated Craig. He was a hard man to know. He lived near us on the Hudson and was a great admirer of Grandma's. She used to say his money was clean because it had been laundered. New money was all right once it found its way into old hands. Craig's father, being a proper Erskine, was permitted, in her mind, to derive his wealth from the lowly Rockefeller. When Grandma died, and he saw that I was alone and poor, he simply proposed to me!"

"You mean he was sorry for you?"

"Well, that was part of it. But not all. I'm going to tell you the whole story, Christopher, because at my age it doesn't matter. And besides, everyone else is dead."

I was silent, in fear that any comment might put her off.

"You don't ask why I accepted him," she pursued. "You think that's too obvious?"

"It's not at all obvious. But you said you would tell me the story."

"Well, sir, the reason I took him is that I loved him! I was in love with a confirmed bachelor of forty, whose eyes lit up only for Watteau and Fragonard! You will say I had no alternative."

"Don't put words in my mouth, Mrs. Erskine."

"Call me Maud. You were fresh enough to call all the others by their first names."

"Maud." My collection was complete!

"I loved him because he was sorry for me. Yes, it was as simple as that — I love his memory to this day because he was sorry for me. And now shall I come to the wedding night?"

"By all means!"

"A man as sophisticated as yourself will not be surprised to hear that nothing happened. Craig had had no experience whatever with women. He had been raised by a tyrannical, puritan, widowed father who made him share his bedroom until he was twenty-five! He was taught to regard women as designing monsters. He was afraid that he would never be able to handle a bride unless she was so old and plain that she would be grateful for any kind of performance! Yet he also believed that with her gratitude he would gain confidence and at last a glorious love."

I stared. "And that happened?"

"That did *not* happen, Christopher. At least in the way you're thinking. Our marriage was never consummated."

So Adeline Bloodgood was not the only virgin of the Book Class! "How did you work it out then?"

"By love," she replied firmly. "Craig was in despair at his incapacity. I think he was even near to suicide. Only when I convinced him that I did not desire a physical union did he begin to regain his spirits and sanity."

"And that was true? That you didn't desire it?"

"Let me put it like this. I desired what he desired. If one sense is shut off, the others become sharper. A blind man feels more keenly with his fingertips. Love that is not expressed physically can be just as fine and just as fulfilling in other ways. Craig and I had as great a marriage as any of the Book Class. Greater, really!"

I contemplated the old girl with delight. For I believed her! I wanted to put my arms around her old skeleton and hug her. But I knew better. Maud Erskine, for all her broadmindedness, had still a good deal of the Book Class in her make-up; she would not have cared for the overdemonstrative gesture. I could simply sit still and be grateful to her for enunciating a doctrine that I had found true in my own life: that love can take many forms and be subject to many divisions. It does not wholly depend on two human beings touching each other. But of course in the grossly corporal age in which we live this will be mocked at. Maud and I are alone.

"People wondered what Craig and I had in common," she continued. "They noted all the superficial things: that his aesthetic pleasure came from pictures and mine from books, that he was dressy and I was dowdy, that he loved parties and I preferred solitude. What they didn't see was that we were perfectly reconciled to our differences and that in foreign posts we complemented each other. He could take care of the grand guests, I of the shy ones. He could train his staff in policy, while I saw that the wives and children had the right houses and schools. Oh, we were a team!"

"You know, it occurs to me that that was what *all* the Class should have been," I intervened. "Wives of diplomats! That was the *one* career they were intellectually and emotionally prepared for. They all wanted to share their husbands' work, and they all knew how to give parties."

"But there's much more to diplomatic life than giving parties," Maud reproved me. "Indeed, parties can be a stumbling block. Craig lost his chance for promotion when he was First Secretary of the embassy in Rome and wouldn't ask to dinner an uncouth Western Senator who was visiting the Eternal City with a large, unattractive wife. The horrid man raised hell when he got back to Washington, and we were confronted with the alternative of taking a minor post or resigning from the service. Craig wanted the latter, but I persuaded him to stay on. After all, I told him, 'It *was* your fault.' So we ate humble pie in small, hot countries for many years. But he was still a Minister before he died."

Minister to Honduras! Still, it was something. But it bothered me that she had made no mention of my manuscript. Had she really hated it?

"Oh, no, I was very much interested," she assured me when I asked. "It would be impossible not to be, knowing them all so well. But you left out a lot of things."

"Such as?"

"Well, you left three of the ladies out altogether. Minnie Gaynor, Nancy Potts and Eloise Le Boutillier. You never even mentioned their names."

"I couldn't think of anything to say about them."

"Because they bored you? Because they had happy marriages and raised scads of children? Are you sure that's not the old bachelor in you coming out? You struck me at times as being almost anti-family, Christopher."

"You can hardly expect me to plead guilty to that. And how do you know who's had a happy marriage, anyway? Your generation was so expert in façades, Maud!"

"That didn't keep you from trying to penetrate Justine's. You went a bit far there. I can't believe that she deliberately ruined her husband's chances for that headmastership."

"How did she do it then?"

"Wouldn't she have tackled him directly? Wouldn't she have told him flatly that he wasn't fit for the job?"

"It's perfectly possible. Of course I was guessing. What else did I get wrong about the Class?"

"Well, you're never going to convince me that Judge Melrose was responsible for Adeline Bloodgood's not marrying. She was always afraid of the least intimacy with men, and she used her worship of the Judge as an excuse. It was better to strike people as a vestal virgin than a compulsive one."

"Mightn't the reader deduce that from my chapter?"

"Then why not say it outright? Why be Jamesian about it? And another thing. I believe your mother cared a good deal more for your father than you let on. Even after that stock business."

"I suppose that's the old bachelor coming out again!"

"*And* the novelist. But you hit one of the gals right on the nose. Leila Lee."

"How you all had it in for her!"

"Because she was the only one who remembered she was a

woman? I liked the way you put that. Much good it did her. The Book Class never used sex as a weapon."

"They used tribalism instead."

Maud shrugged. "Why should they have used anything? Who was their enemy? Maybe they *would* have been better off in businesses or professions, like the young women today. Georgia and Justine would have certainly got on. Perhaps even Polly Travers."

"And yourself, of course."

"Well, diplomacy *was* a sort of career for wives. In my day, anyway. Do you think your mother'd have been happy running a real estate agency? Or Genevieve teaching school? Who knows? As you say, those girls had many privileges. But privileges don't always make for happiness."

"What shall I say about the Class by way of conclusion? How can I sum them up?"

Maud thought for a time. She closed her eyes, and for a moment I thought she had gone to sleep.

"By repeating what you said in your first chapter," she answered at last, sitting up. "That they were serious."

"Serious about what?"

"About their mission in life. Whatever it was."

"Even Leila?"

"Well, as you pointed out, she was serious about men. And Mylo was serious about one man, her husband. And your mother was determined to be the best banker's daughter and wife in town. It wasn't all men, either. Georgia wanted to stimulate people into being good citizens. Polly worried about our souls. Genevieve tried to give France back to the Bourbons, and Justine . . . well, Justine wanted to do every-thing better than anyone else! Oh, you can laugh at them, but they didn't waste their lives. They didn't throw away that precious gift, as so many people do. They knew they were supposed to be privileged, and they thought that placed them under some kind of duty."

"To be what?"

"To be good!" Maud's shrug was monumental. "Don't ask me whether they succeeded. I don't know! And, anyway, it's your project, not mine."

"I suppose it's appropriate that the Book Class should end in a book." I saw that she was tired now, and I rose to take my leave. "Even if it has to be a book of mine."

Walking home that evening, I wondered whether I had shed any light on the question that I had originally posed. Just what *was* the "power" of the Book Class? Had it, in the last analysis, been wielded effectively only upon myself? Was it, other than that, a figment of my imagination?

I decided that I did not know, but that I could make one small affirmation. Those women continued to occupy an unduly large space in the reflections and fantasies of their surviving children.

Chuck Bannard likes nothing better than to talk about his mother, and the good and bad she may have done to him, over long drinks at the Patroons. Alida, Mylo's daughter, has waxed rather cloyingly sentimental about the parent whose extravagance she deplored in her lifetime. Margot Travers goes to see her mother every day in the nursing home. And Manny and Eleanor and I have our only really pleasant and congenial conversations exchanging anecdotes and memories about Mother.

What would the Book Class say if *this* book came up for discussion at lunch on a fleecy cloud above?

I can hear Adeline's wail: "How could darling Christopher be so undarling? He *knew* I never wanted that interview with

Uncle Luke to be published. But even that's nothing compared with what Maud said about me! Oh, I tell you, when she gets up here at last, she's going to have a piece of my mind!"

And Genevieve, pensively: "How *awful* my sister-in-law was. Imagine saying those things about her own nephew. Was I the only Terrasson who cared about the family?"

Leila (from a lower cloud): "Isn't it odd, Genevieve, that after eight centuries their principal defender should come from a Yankee department store? What fascinated *me* was what Maud had to say about her own marriage. I always suspected that was *un peu blanc!*"

Now Polly: "I guess I'll never understand God. When he took such care with his own Gospels, why did he leave me to an evangelist like Christopher?"

Mylo: "*I* can't complain. He put in only what I gave him."

Justine: "I gave him nothing! He had to make up what he said about me."

Georgia: "Well, you must admit he was at least interested in us. I'd rather be slandered than forgotten. Do you suppose when *he* gets here — if the wretch ever makes it — we might have a party and let him read aloud selected parts of the book?"

Cornelia: "Never! It is all very well for the rest of you, but how do you think *I* feel? My own son making such a goose of me!"

But surely, dearest Mother, if you have another life, it is one where such things are understood! I couldn't bear even to think of this little book if that were not the case. For everything I have said has been said with love. There are those, I suppose, who will not believe that I know what love is. They are wrong. Everyone knows what love is. It is life.

*The Book Class* has been set in Linotype Janson, a recutting of the original type cut between 1660 and 1687 by Anton Janson, a Leipzig punchcutter and typefounder. The heirs of Janson and his successor, Edling, brought the matrices to Holland, where they were purchased by the Stempel foundry. The linotype recutting was made from type cast from these original matrices. Display type is handset foundry Caslon Openface.

Composition by Maryland Linotype
Composition Co., Inc.